IN
LOVE AND
WATER

CURTIS MAYNARD
Author of *The* Rose Diary

CHAPTER ONE

I settled down in a green chair near the swimming pool and heaved a huge sigh of relief when my back finally rested well against the chair. I could not believe sitting down had become a chore for me, as I could hear my bone make cracking noises whenever I moved around nowadays. I had never thought about becoming old, and now I knew I had no choice but to think about it. I would be sixty-nine in a few days, and reality was starting to dawn on me. My joints no longer moved freely without me feeling pains, and my hair was no longer as it used to be, very long and curly. I now had a tuff of grey hair with my edges receding backward each day; I kept a beard that made me look like an ancient wizard. My skin was wrinkly and folded up in some corners.

I often blamed age for taking away my youthful beauty, and the only thing that remained the same about me was my eyes. I had worry lines at each side of my lips, but my eyes still felt the same as I could even see better now than twenty years ago. They were the color of the sea, and they looked like someone had soaked them in water. Also, since my eyes were the only thing that decided not to age, they seemed to hold a lot of secrets. I often looked like someone who was carrying the weight of the world in his eyes; well, so I have been told. People had often stopped on the road when they saw my eyes. Their faces would automatically be moved with compassion and pity that often made me very uncomfortable; this was why I had decided to get glasses even if I did not need them.

The glasses only made me look older and wiser, and I often laughed at the mirror when I saw my reflection in it. My mouth never smiled, and I was often referred to as the grumpy old man. I did not understand how some people always had a smile on their faces. I usually called them pretenders as I believed no one was truly ever happy. I had expected my voice to change when I got older, and I assumed that was how things worked when you grew older. However, I was very disappointed when the reverse was the case. I had been born with a very tiny voice, and when puberty hit, it remained the same, and now my voice was still the same even in my old age.

I was currently seated by a swimming pool; it had only seemed right for me to return to the place where it all started, the place where I had lost so much and given so much to. I stared at the swimming pool and watched as the water glistered under my watchful eyes. There was no one with me as I had paid to have the place to myself for the day; I did not understand why I had to go there that day. I had been having a lot of sleepless nights at that time. It was as if my past had finally come back to haunt me with full force. I had tried taking my sleeping pills, but that had only made things worse for me. I had been unable to sleep throughout the day before and had no choice but to drive down there that day.

My past was something I had buried so deep down inside me that I never gave it any chance to resurface. However, as I looked at the pool that day, the memories came rushing back like a gust of wind. My mind took me back to my childhood before life dealt me a severe blow in the face. I had grown up in a little town in Denver; my parents had conceived me before they got married. My mother Sarah had been born into a wealthy family; she had gone to the best schools and had gotten the most pleasing things money could ever buy. She had snuck out of her house to attend a pool party on the day she met my father. My father, David, had been the lifeguard at the pool party, and his job had been to watch over drunken college students and prevent them from drowning.

David had been doing his job diligently until he got pushed into the pool by Sarah's friends. He was so annoyed and embarrassed the moment it happened that he stormed off angrily after getting out of the water. Sarah ran after him that day to apologize for her friends' behavior, and they bonded after that. Their relationship was one Sarah's parents never agreed upon because David was not from a wealthy family; however, this did not stop my parents from pursuing a relationship with each other. My mother discovered she was pregnant with me a few days after her college graduation and was too terrified to tell her parents. However, she told my dad and had expected him to react differently than he did that day as he jumped for joy in happiness. He was so supportive of her and urged her to tell her parents. On the other hand, my grandparents were not so happy that their only child had been knocked up by some guy with no shares or investments to his name.

They gave my mother an ultimatum and had asked her to pick between traveling to Europe to have me while she married a wealthy billionaire's son and staying in the United States with my father and being cut out of their lives forever. My mother was heartbroken when she heard this and was unable to come to terms with being disowned by her parents.

She chose to stay with my father in the United States, as a result of which she was sent out of the house with nothing but her trust fund. My grandparents had been generous enough to have saved so much for her in her trust fund that all my parents' fears vanished when they saw the amount of money they had.

My grandparents traveled to London a month after my mother moved in with my dad. My mother told me that they were so scared of what society would think of them that they absconded the moment it became apparent that she was pregnant and not just adding weight.

My mother had gone to see if she could withdraw her trust fund immediately after her parents left when she realized she had to be twenty-two years old before she could do that. According to my dad, she was heartbroken and depressed for the first three months of her pregnancy. He was unable to cheer her up, and this only made things worse for their relationship. My dad was working two shifts at that time so they could prepare for my birth. Things were very difficult for them at that time, and they had days when they could not afford to eat three square meals. My mother was always scared I was going to come out malnourished.

Few months before my due date, my mother began to develop so many pregnancy complications, and ninety percent of the money my dad made went into paying the hospital bills. My mother never got the luxury of eating anything she craved when she was pregnant with me and only ate a limited amount of food each day. She was also unable to work during her pregnancy, and this frustrated her more. My mother was not an idle person, and she would often cry herself to sleep whenever she realized she really could not do anything about it. The week before my arrival on this planet called Earth, my mother had finally come to terms with the reality of her situation. The money she had saved while in college was used to buy a baby crib and clothes for me. She was very selective in the things she bought because she did not want to use up all the money before I arrived.

My mother had been cleaning my soon-to-be nursery the moment her water broke; she had assumed it was pee and had cleaned it up and continued with what she was doing. It was when the first contraction hit that she panicked. She had heard pregnancy rumors, but she had never really expected it to be that painful. When she told me this story, she was very dramatic as she claimed the reason she was giving me such explicit details of my birth was because she wanted me to value women.

When my mother arrived at Greenwood hospital, she was placed in a ward with women who had also had their waters broken, the whole place terrified her and she became very anxious. They shared funny pregnancy experiences to keep their minds off their contractions, and little by little they were able to find laughter even amid their pain. Although my mother had heard wonderful stories from the women who were in the ward with her, she was still terrified about becoming a mother. Her own pregnancy journey had been the worst, and she was more excited at the prospect of meeting me than anything else.

My dad arrived before the second contraction came around and he was sweating profusely as he had run up the stairs instead of taking the elevator. My mother later told me he looked way worse than she did. He held my mother's hands, and they both watched together how some women were moved to another ward because their labor had become more active. My parents both watched in fear as this happened; my mother claimed that my father felt like fleeing the ward when he saw a woman go crazy on her husband. She cursed him and blamed him for putting her in the situation she was currently in. When the second wave of pain came, it lasted for thirty minutes, and my mother successfully crushed my father's fingers as she held them tight. She had expected the pain to be similar to menstrual pain at least because that was what my great-grandmother had told her.

My mother became jealous of women who were being wheeled into the labor room and she wondered why I was taking my time. I guess she finally found out the answer to this question five years later. My mother had been scared she was going to give birth in the toilet and had tried her best to hold her pee in, she had read up on a lot of pregnancy books that had made her believe that she could push me out while she peed. My dad also panicked so much during my mother's contraction that he was sent out of the wardroom. He had raised two false alarms by pretending he had seen my head poking out of my mother's dress. To this day I still do not get how anyone bought such a lie in the first place.

I came into the world on the 15th of March. I had made my mother so restless for two days that she had finally given up on me arriving that day. She had spent two nights in the hospital and was on the verge of losing her mind when the doctor suggested she came back when the contractions become more intense. My mother was very sad as she was leaving the hospital; she had badly wanted to hold me in her arms, and I still want to believe that I must have felt her sadness because she no longer had to leave the hospital. I decided to grace the world with my presence at that moment. My mother was rushed into the labor room, and the doctor in charge of her delivery called what happened that day a miracle.

I began to cry as soon as my head came out of my mother's vagina; it was as if I already knew I was coming into an unfair world. I was a very healthy baby, and this made my mother extra proud of herself. They named me Kendrick that day just because both of my parents were fans of Kendrick Lamar. My parents never called me Kendrick again, they preferred to call me Ken, and everyone did. My parents sent a picture of me to my grandparents, but they still never reached out.

CHAPTER TWO

Two years after I was born, my mother became eligible to collect her trust fund. It was the happiest day of her life. She worked in a small coffee shop in our neighborhood as she wanted a job where she could take me along. The money gotten from the job was used to complement my father's salary since he also got a new job a few weeks after I was born. We were not rich, but we survived, and this was why getting my mother's trust fund was the best news to have happened to my family. My parents planned for months how they were going to spend the money. My mother received yet more shocking news when she went to the bank on that fateful day; she was told the money had doubled and that she had up to thirty million dollars in her account. She did not know how that was possible, but she felt her parents must have had something to do with it. On my part, I saw it as an attempt to acknowledge my existence because my mother immediately opened a trust fund for me too that day.

My second day was a day of celebration for my parents; my dad quit his job as planned and we all set out to celebrate. My parents had always enjoyed swimming and this was something they never got to do because of the nature of their jobs.

I remember this day so well because it was the beginning of my doom. When my dad placed me in my brand-new stroller, I loved how blue the sky was and I cried so loud when my mother tried to take me out of the stroller. I remember how a woman came to tell my mother that babies were not allowed in that section of the pool. My mother immediately became sad but complied and took me to the kiddies' poolside. When we got there, a swimming instructor asked my parents if they would like me to learn how to swim, and they answered yes. I was very reluctant to leave my mother's arms, and I cried even more when she tried to pass me over to the swimming instructor.

"He doesn't like strangers," my mother told the swimming instructor in her kind voice.

"Do you swim? Maybe you could guide him if you can," the instructor suggested.

My mother nodded, and she was given a floater for me. The floater was shaped like a duck; still, I dodged all attempts to wear it. It never occurred to me that I created a scene that day, yet I remember people stopped to look at what I was doing.

"He can swim without it as long as we both guide him," the swimming instructor told my mother, who was oblivious to the fact that people were watching her.

I clung to my mother's dress tightly before my feet finally touched the water. As I felt the water's coldness on my feet, I struggled out of my mother's hold in excitement and began to go down. I could hear the piercing screams of my mother's voice resonating through the water. She assumed I was drowning, and almost all the lifeguards stationed by the pool jumped into the water to save me. I wonder where they later were when I needed them in the future. The number of hands I saw trying to grab me that day terrified me, and I was unaware of when my legs began to move of their own accord. I started playing with the water, moving my hands and legs as I discovered that my movement seemed to propel me forward. I decided to continue flapping my hands like a fish, and the water also seemed to make me happy. I remember looking up and discovering that no hand tried to grab me again; I searched for my mother but could not find her.

That was the moment I began to panic and the first time I shed tears. However, it was not the last time because I soon found my mother beside me when I started wailing. She held me and looked at me in awe. As she took me to where everyone else was, I began to wonder what had happened. People were gathered around the poolside, and they were holding their phones and cameras. This made my mother so uncomfortable that she had to wrap me in a yellow blanket. The blanket was very warm, and I snuggled inside comfortably. As I slept soundly in our new car that day, I did not wake or stir all through the car ride and even slept into the next day while refusing to eat dinner. My parents worried that I had fallen sick that day and constantly checked up on me.

The next day, my parents were very happy when I did not end up running a temperature. As I took my bath in our new large bathtub, which was filled with toys and bubbles, I became so excited to have my bath that I did not mind getting scrubbed with a washcloth by my mother. I was also very reluctant to leave the bathroom that day, and it took my father's intervention before I agreed to come out of the bathtub. We ate breakfast in our new home for the first time. Our new home was exquisite; my parents had already made their choice and spoken to the real estate agent before the money came into their hands. My mother had also gone furniture shopping to pick the furniture she would like to have delivered. My parents did not allow any wind of doubt to come near them, and they had shopped and planned for this even before getting the money. When the money finally came, everything was just as rosy as anticipated.

We moved into our new house the same day my mother got her money; they had even hired an interior decorator days before the big move. My parents had always been the best at organizing, and this saved me a lot of wasted time while growing up. The house my parents bought was a two-story building located in one of those lavish areas. The house consisted of four rooms and a huge playground. I still believe my mother bought the home because of the playground that had caught her attention and not the room or kitchen size. We all dined together at our new dining table, and I remember how precious the moment was to my little self, such that I was very excited. While we ate that morning, my parents' phone also seemed to ring nonstop. At first they decided to leave it unattended so we could enjoy our first breakfast as a family. However, the person on the other end of the line had an intense purpose as the phone kept on ringing.

My father was forced to leave the table and go for the phone; when he returned, he looked like he was taken aback by something. He stared at me for so long that I began to fuss in my chair. After ten minutes of silence, my father finally found his voice again. My very worried mother had assumed the worst already and looked ready to call the hospital.

"They want Ken to come on their show," my father informed my mother.

"What show? Who are they?" my mother asked, even more confused at that point.

"The NBBC," my father replied.

"The NBBC? What do they want Ken on their show for?"

"They said they saw his swimming video and they would like us to talk about his love for swimming."

"But he has never swum before; that was his first time. Did you tell them that?"

"Yes, I did. That only seemed to make them more interested," my father said in awe.

My parents remained silent for over an hour that day as they thought about what to do. Then finally they agreed to take me to the interview; this was something we all eventually decided was a wrong move as the years went by.

On the day of the interview, my mother dressed me up in a little baby suit. I still have the picture; my mother loved it so much that I have since then not been able to burn it or throw it away.

The interview room was brightly colored, and I remember how much everyone wanted to take pictures of me. My dad held my hands that day, and I remember vividly how sweaty his palms were. He was not used to things like that, unlike my mother, who looked like she was born for the camera. She dressed the part and acted it perfectly. I, too, busily stared at my shoes that lit up whenever I walked and did not notice the eyes that were staring at me.

"How long has your son been swimming?" This was the first question the interviewer asked my dad. The interviewer was a slim woman with long curly hair. She had a perfect set of teeth and seemed to measure her smiles before letting them out. She had asked my father this question before the interview began, and my dad wondered why she asked him again. My mother came in when she realized that my father was not going to talk. At some point in the interview, I could also sense the sudden change in my mother's tone as the interviewer kept trying to bait her. The interviewer was named Becky, and she tried to make my parents look like liars. She spent half of the interview period trying to make them admit to having taken me to swimming lessons before.

"No, that was his first time. We were both as shocked as everyone," my mother told her in a resigned tone.

Becky finally agreed with my mother, and at this point in the interview, she tried to ask me questions. As she asked me questions about starting a career as a swimmer, my mother found her just so weird. That day, as we left the building, my mother promised that there would be no more interviews, but this was not true as there were more to come.

CHAPTER THREE

My newfound fame as the outstanding swimmer child eventually got the attention of the mayor. His visit was something my parents never expected. They were planning the establishment of their new business when the mayor came knocking. My mother told me that her hair was tied up in a messy bun and she was still in a bathrobe. My father was also just dressed in his shorts and an oversized shirt while I was in my playpen. The mayor came with his camera crew and gave my parents the chance to change into something more presentable before the cameras started rolling. This, however, did not help wipe the shock off my parents' faces.

As my mother brought me before the presence of the mayor, I cried when I saw him. I was not too fond of the fact that he had interrupted my playtime, and I only stopped crying when I was given a huge shiny toy to play with by the mayor's personal assistant. On that day, my parents conducted another interview with the mayor against their earlier resolution. Subsequent to this, I was given a scholarship to study in a swimming school after high school, and all my tuition was paid for. They also proposed to erect a pool in our backyard that day. I was given a swimming coach, and my life was planned out for me.

The rain fell heavily overnight and did not stop even when it was morning. This prevented the pool builders from coming to erect a swimming pool as they could not work under the rain. It rained for two days nonstop. I still believe that the universe was trying to tell us all something at this point, but my parents did not listen. They even started to warm up to the idea of having their own private pool in the house, and my mother wondered why she had not thought of it before.

On the day the rain stopped, the pool builders came to install the pool in our backyard; they came so early in the morning that I wondered why they were so excited to work. It took them just a day to create a very large swimming pool in our backyard. When I first laid my eyes on it, I immediately fell in love with it; but, as they say, love fades away and dies. My parents felt so happy that we all took a swim in the pool. There was a deep side created for my parents and a shallow side for me. A long thick rope demarcated the deep side, and my parents were reassured, knowing that there was no way I would be able to get to that side. I watched my mother swim that day and copied everything she did; it was as though I had a photographic memory when it came to swimming.

A man came the next day to our house when we had all gone out to check my parents' new office space. When we came back, the man was seated near our doorstep; he jumped up on his feet and introduced himself as Arnold, my new swimming instructor. My parents had forgotten about him coming over and apologized profusely as they welcomed him to our house. When I first saw Arnold, I assumed he would be a mean person, and I followed my parents around the house that day to avoid being alone with him. He had a huge scar on his face that made him look mean whenever he was not smiling; he also had a very deep voice that scared me on countless occasions. He was a tall man and looked like he should have been playing for the NBA. Also, he was very muscular. He dressed up in a very corporate wear, but actually this was the only day he did so. Wearing a suit had never been his thing, and I think I must have imbibed such non-suit-wearing culture from him.

"My name is Coach Arnold."

This was the first thing he said to me as he bent down to hold my tiny fingers. He then smiled at me and asked my mother to lead us to the pool.

"I want to see what he can do," Arnold told my mother when we got to the pool.

My mother looked at him with one eyebrow raised, confused as to what he really wanted to see. She had gotten my little Power Rangers swim shorts and helped me put them on. She followed me inside the water and cheered me on to swim.

"You can do it," she cheered happily as she noticed I was not moving.

Coach Arnold advised my mother to get out of the water and bring me out along with her. He instructed her to give us some privacy so we could talk man to man. I really did not expect my mother to do such a thing, but she bent down and kissed my forehead before walking inside. When my mother left, Coach Arnold bent down to my height and told me a story about the courageous baby frog who had swum in a big ocean without any fear.

I became so engrossed in the story the coach told me that I became sad when it ended. The story about the baby frog was meant to boost my bravery, but what it had done to me instead was show me that Coach Arnold was a nice person. I went back into the water alone that day and swam my best under the watchful eyes of Coach Arnold. I showed him what I learned from my mother the previous day, and that seemed to impress him because he gave me a thumbs up as I came out of the water. My parents must have been proud of me for some reason because they allowed me to play with my action figures for a very long time that day before asking me to go to bed. This only made me excited for the next visit of Coach Arnold, and I even attributed my parents' happiness to his arrival.

The next few months passed by in a blur and I can hardly remember anything else from that time. I remember beginning school a few months after we settled down in our new house. I also excelled in my swimming lessons with Coach Arnold, and he even nicknamed me the fish. My parents' business also took off as my mother used her skills as a business administrator to build something special for her and my dad. They bought a whole building and transformed it into a bakery and a gadgets store. The bakery was for my mother while the gadget store was for my father. My mother made the bakery my favorite place in the world as she always spoiled me with treats whenever I went there. Her bakery always smelt of butter and made my mouth water whenever I walked into it; it was very homely and even had a fireplace where people could warm up during the winter or on rainy days. Everyone loved my mother's bakery because it was also a place where people often came to relax and catch up with their friends. Her bakery was called Home Away from Home and this was the perfect name for her store since she had really put her hundred percent in it. She had also hired the best staff. My father's store was also ranked number one in the whole town just a few months after it took off. There was good news flowing from all directions, and I was delighted to know that my parents were happy.

Two years passed before the sweetest blessing was given to my parents. My mother became pregnant again and made my dad the happiest man on Earth once again. When she told me the news, I immediately felt sad because I had not been ready to share my parents with anybody. However, I later became very happy when I realized that I could now have someone to train with. My mother's pregnancy was stress-free, she was able to work each day in her bakery, and the only times she visited the hospital were when she went for her antenatal and my sister's delivery. The day of my sister's birth still remains the best day of my life. I had been an eager five-year-old boy who wondered if my mother's stomach was going to burst open like a watermelon before my sister would come out. Once my mother's water had broken, I was there to help her mop the floor thinking my sister would come out like water and become an ice girl. My ridiculous question was even able to distract my mother from the pain she was experiencing at that time as she tried to explain to me how babies were born.

My dad rushed back home to take my mother to the hospital. I begged to follow them, but they refused and dropped me off with Mr. Greg, our neighbor. Mr. Greg had a grandchild named Kevin, who I loved playing with, but on the day of my sister's birth, I was not interested in playing with anybody until I met her.

"You are now a big brother, Ken," Mr. Greg told me that day after getting off the phone with my parents.

I became very happy with my new status, and I excitedly waited for my parents and sister to come back that day. They had even allowed me to pick her name, but I had not yet told them what it would be. I was super excited, and I watched the clock tick slowly while poking my head behind the curtains to check if my parents were back yet. By midnight Mr. Greg received another call from my parents telling him that they would not be able to come back that same night as my sister still needed to be watched. I was scared and feared the worst when I heard them speak to me on the phone; I remember how I cried because I felt the doctor would take my sister away from me. My tired mother, however, was able to reassure me over the phone that everything was fine.

The next day, I woke up before everyone else in anticipation of my sister's arrival. When I heard my father's honk as they drove down the driveway, I ran like my pants were on fire. Mr. Greg screamed for me to slow down, but I turned a deaf ear to his cries and found my way to our house all by myself. When I got to our house, I could see my father smiling from his side-view mirror as he got out of the car. I briefly hugged him and waited for him to open the car door for my mother. As the door was swung open, my eyes zoomed in on the sleeping figure in my mother's arms. It was my sister, and she was the most beautiful person I had ever laid my eyes on; she had a curly mass of hair on her head, and her hands were curled up in a fist as though she was about to throw a punch. It was as if she sensed me by her side because her eyes fluttered open like a butterfly's wing. She had deep-colored brown eyes that reminded me of my favorite cereal, and I was totally captivated by them. No one said a word as we all just looked at her.

"Say hello to your sister," my mother finally told me as she pressed a very cold hand sanitizer into my hands and then cleaned it with a wipe.

I was so scared to touch her; still, my fingers found their way to her tiny little ones. She grabbed my finger immediately her hand came in contact with mine and wrapped all five fingers around my one. This single act alone made me promise myself always to protect her as my innocent baby sister.

"So, what did you decide to name your sister?" My dad, who I had forgotten about, asked from behind me.

"Star! Her name is Star because she makes us all happy, just like the stars in the sky."

After I said this, my mother became very teary, and I also started crying because I thought I had said something wrong. My father ended up laughing at the two of us, and we all moved inside as the happy family that we were.

That night was one of the best nights ever. I stayed up with my mother and helped hold Star whenever she cried. That night, I dreamt of someone taking her away from me and immediately I woke up from sleep; I ran to my parents' room to check if she was still there or had really disappeared.

I also refused to go to school and wondered why everyone got to stay at home with my new baby sister except me. It took a lot of convincing and bribery on the part of my parents before I eventually decided to go to school. When I got to school, I greeted my pre-school teacher Miss Lauren and told her about the birth of my sister, I was actually hoping that she would allow me to go back home, but she did not. I became very unable to pay attention in class that day as my body was full of excitement to go home. When the bell rang that day for our closure, I was the first person to fly out of my chair. My teacher excused my hyperactivity that day as she understood that I was only acting that way because of my sister Star. When my dad came to pick me up from school that afternoon, he allowed me to ride with him in the front. He made a short detour by visiting the store first; this annoyed me so much because, as much as I loved my parents' store, I had not planned on visiting there that day. I grumbled loudly when asked to come out of the car; my father, who was not expecting my displeasure at being in the store, allowed me to touch some of the gadgets in there to appease me. I also got to eat my favorite chocolate chip cookies from my mother's bakery, which helped calm my anger down more. Finally, my dad announced that it was time for us to go, and the smile I had kept buried ever since we got to the store returned.

I tried to bounce in my seat as we neared my house, but the seatbelt I had been strapped in limited such action. As I got inside my house, I noticed that we had a few visitors. I started feeling sad that our house was occupied with people I really did not want to see at that point. I said a quick hello to everybody before I dashed for my mother's room. When I got to my mother's room, she was nowhere to be found, but my sister slept soundly in her crib. I tiptoed around her crib, careful enough not to wake her up, and watched her sleep till I felt sleepy and made myself comfortable on my parents' bed.

I felt someone tug on my hair gently as I slept, and my eyes immediately snapped open. The first thing I saw as I opened my eyes was my baby sister Star, and she was lying face down on my parents' bed with my mother sitting in a protective way around her. She had a small lock of my hair in her hand, and she pulled it immediately she noticed that I was awake.

She looked at me just the way an owl looked at people, and then she smiled when I touched her little toes. I played with my sister that day and told her about our parents' store. I didn't care if she understood a thing I said but continued talking to her until she started crying because she was hungry. I asked my mother why Star could not share my spaghetti and meatballs, and she explained to me in detail the difference between baby food and adult food. I did not understand anything she told me that day, but I was very grateful that my mother took the time to answer all my questions.

CHAPTER FIVE

The next day, Coach Arnold came around for my training. I took him to meet Star, and he also loved her immediately he saw her. My mother and father, in fact, made Arnold my sister's godfather, and I could see that she had already wrapped her hands around his finger. Coach Arnold had become more than a friend to us ever since I started training with him, and he took me to my first swimming competition at the age of four. He stood by me when I won my first medal as a little boy and was still the first person to say he was proud of me before my parents. He was also the first person I told when I had been picked on in the locker room because of my size and age. I was privileged to compete in the junior category and represented my town at just the age of four; most boys who competed in the race were between eight and nine. They all assumed I did not know how to swim because of my size and age and had picked on me continuously till I ran screaming for Coach Arnold just like they wanted. Coach Arnold had reported them to an official, but nothing was done about it; thus, I entered the locker room more scared than ever. When I got inside, I saw all of them staring at me like I had grown seven heads. I already knew at that point that they must have heard about the news of me reporting them. As I neared them, I saw one of the boys point a finger, and I already knew the bullying would start again.

They called me all sorts of names that day, but I did not care because Coach Arnold had told me I was the best and that the only reason they were picking on me was because they were scared I was going to beat them in the competition. My tear ducts paid no regard to this as I became teary and just found my way to the shower. It was on my way to the shower that I met a boy named Lance. Lance looked almost as small as I was, and I wondered if he was my age mate. I got scared at first when he walked towards me because I assumed he wanted to continue the bullying I had walked away from, but the reverse was the case.

"Hi, my name is Lance," he had said as he stretched his hands forward.

"My name is K ... en, Ken," I answered between sniffles.

"Do not mind those boys. They are just afraid of you," Lance told me.

Hearing those words from Lance only proved that Coach Arnold's words true. I knew the two of them could not have practiced a lie together, and so I dried up my tears immediately. Lance helped me turn the shower knob since my hands were unable to reach it, and we both talked about which color of power rangers we liked best. We soon heard a whistle blow indicating that it was time for the swimmers to walk out, and we did just that. When I got outside, I was terrified when I saw the large crowd that had come to watch us swim. I did not realize that people enjoyed swimming as a sport that much; my legs became wobbly, and I scanned the crowd for my parents. When I couldn't see them, I immediately became sad.

"Your mother and dad are running late. They are delayed

in traffic. I am sure they will be here soon, so chin up and smile," Coach Arnold had said.

He took my hands and led me towards the poolside. When we got there, I noticed how large the swimming pool was. It was twice as big as the one in our house, and I began wondering if I would be able to swim in such a big pool. Coach Arnold, however, did not allow such fear to find room in my head as he talked me out of my fear and promised to take me for ice cream if I won. I was certainly a lover of ice cream, and since Coach Arnold had never taken me out for anything, it was really going to be a big one for me. I was left alone when the race was about to start as we were all asked to take our places in the specific boxes marked for us. The bottom of the water had our numbers marked on it, and we had been instructed to follow the path our numbers were on.

As I looked at the crowd one more time, hoping to see my parents, I began to feel sad till I saw my name on cardboard with shiny power rangers saying, "You can do it." I immediately knew it was my parents, and I felt better knowing that they were around. We were all asked to take our stance while waiting for the sound of the whistle. I looked at the water like I had been instructed to and immediately I heard the whistle's sound, I jumped inside it. It was a wonderful feeling as the only person I had ever competed with were my parents and Coach Arnold. I swam effortlessly and reached the finish line under five seconds; Coach Arnold had made me circle our pool for that short amount of time every day so this was a piece of cake to me.

When I got out, I realized I was the only one out, and the whole place was silent. It was as if no one could believe that someone my size could swim that fast. I could hear the fast rhythm of my heartbeat as I wondered why everyone was quiet. It was when Lance came out next after eleven seconds that they realized I swam with people. The commentator marveled at my excellent swimming skills, and I was praised. The crowd went wild when the other older kids came out of the water, maybe they must thought I had murdered them because their surprise that day was great. I was given my first gold medal on that day and also made my first few enemies too. Some parents tried to find ways to discredit my winning and even said that I was too small to compete. However, my dad and Coach Arnold were there to help fight for my winning, which only angered these parents. That day, my father and mother were so proud of me, and Coach Arnold also fulfilled his promise of buying me ice cream. He got me a very large ice cream he knew I could not finish.

CHAPTER SIX

The cloud was pregnant with rain on the day my grandparents visited. On that day, my sister Star had begun teething again, so she cried every hour until she looked very red. She was not quite two but very smart, and I had taught her my school work because I wanted her to join my class whenever she began school. No one complained about what I did, and so I continued to do it every day. My sister and I were like twins. She always followed me everywhere I went, and I allowed her to do so. It was my name she called first when she started talking; I danced and danced that day, and I knew my parents were jealous because she had not said either of their names. In school, whenever I was asked who my best friend was, I would tell them my sister. Those who did not have sisters were jealous of me and how much I talked about my sister. Yet, this did not stop me from doing so.

My grandparents were not as old as I had expected them to look when they arrived. My grandmother did not have wrinkly skin like I was made to think all grandparents had. She also did not need a cane to walk, nor did she shake like I had seen Mr. Greg shake on some occasions. She was dressed in a very tight blue blazer embedded with shiny pearls and wore a blue skirt to match the blazer. On the other hand, my grandfather was more casually dressed in khaki pants and a blue shirt that had little flamingos on it. They looked different from each other; my grandfather was tall while my grandmother was average height. My grandfather wore a permanent smile on his face, but my grandmother looked incapable of smiling. When I opened the door for them on their arrival, it was my grandmother who spoke first.

"Go and fetch Sarah," she said.

I was baffled as to who Sarah was, and thus I remained rooted to the ground. It was not until my grandfather spoke that I moved; my grandmother just stared at me like I was an alien who could not comprehend what she was saying.

"We are your grandparents," my grandfather said as he stooped down to my height and hugged me.

I became so excited to hear this that I closed the door on them and ran to tell my mother. I still remember how disgusted my grandmother became when I did that.

"Mother, Mother, Mother... Grandpa and Grandma are here," I screamed as I ran towards my parents' room.

My mother was trying to make my sister sleep by singing her a song with her very melodious singing voice.

"What did you just say?" she asked immediately as I walked into the room.

"I said Grandpa and Grandma are here," I said.

My mother just looked at me as if I was speaking another language and then began to laugh.

"Your grandparents are in London. I have told you this before, Ken."

"But there are people at the door who are saying that they are my grandparents; the woman even called you Sarah."

My mother almost dropped Star on the ground just as I

finished my sentence. I decided to collect my sister from her hands because I saw how disoriented she looked already. She immediately called my father to tell him, and they talked for a while before my mother decided to go downstairs. When my mother opened the door, she took a moment to look at her parents' faces as they stood at the doorway before she slammed it shut in their faces again. She looked like she had seen a ghost, and I became scared that I had done something wrong by opening the door to those people in the first place. After about a few seconds, my mother summoned the courage to open the door again, and my grandparents immediately walked in, not taking any chances of having the door slammed in their faces again.

"Is slamming the door in your visitors' faces a norm in your house, Sarah?" my grandmother asked with a stern voice.

My mother looked like she was on the verge of crying, and I had never seen her look so timid in her life. I had to wonder why a mother would want to make her daughter cry.

"Welcome, Mother, welcome, Dad," my mother said when she finally got herself together and showed her parents to their rooms. My grandmother did not bother to acknowledge Star or me, but my grandfather did. He told me that he had bought me a car and also gotten a gift for Star. I liked him all the more after he said this. My grandmother, on the other hand, just scoffed and made her way to her room. Their butler followed closely behind them like a robot, making Star giggle.

My dad arrived hurriedly from the store; he looked very flustered as he dropped his green work bag on the couch and hurried up the stairs to find my mother. I did not know the backstory of what had transpired between my grandparents and my mother, so I wondered why my parents looked more flustered than excited to see them. I took Star to my room, and we both watched television before my parents announced that lunch was ready. When I got downstairs, I was shocked at the amount of food I saw. I asked my father if it was someone's birthday, and he laughed it off. My mother also gave me a beautiful plate to eat with, and I could see my face in its glittery surface. My grandparents joined us at the dining table thirty minutes after lunch was ready, and I was already agitated at their delay because I was starving. When they arrived at the table, I could see that my grandparents' butler had taken over my mother's job of serving us food. I was very tense as my grandparents' butler served the food because my mother would become sad if the table cloth got stained. This was the main reason why she asked my dad and me not to dish our food by ourselves because our hands were always bound to spill something. Lunch was a three-course meal; we had a chicken soup first filled with vegetables that I hated; then we later had green rice with a purple cabbage stew and finally my favorite cake, which was a strawberry cake.

"So, how old are you?" my grandmother asked as she turned to face me.

I was very startled when she turned to face me because I thought she had caught me imitating the way she ate.

"I am seven years old."

"You are a man already. Have you thought about what you would like to major in at the university? "my grandmother asked, still keeping a straight face.

My mother choked on her meal when this question was asked, while my father simply stared at her as though she was crazy.

"Never mind your grandmother. I heard you love swimming?" my grandfather asked.

"Yes, I do, sir. We have a pool too."

"Wow ... that is nice. Maybe you can show me a few swimming tricks when we have rested after this meal."

My mother smiled in appreciation of my grandfather.

"I have medals too, and trophies," I added happily.

This statement I made seemed to catch my grandmother's attention.

"How many do you have?" she asked.

"S-Seven," I said, stammering.

"That is good but not good enough." My grandmother said while looking me in the eye.

"Mother, that is enough," my mother said and pulled me away from the table while I was still eating my strawberry cake.

"But I am not done, Mother," I grumbled as she asked me to go and check on my sister.

I did not return downstairs, so I still had no clue as to what transpired between my mother and my grandparents that day. I was satisfied when my mother came back with my cake and also a tiny slice for my sister who had woken up. I did not bother to ask any questions, and I ate my cake happily.

The next day, things seemed different in the house. I walked downstairs to see my parents smiling alongside my grandmother. Star was with my grandfather, and he was telling her a story when I walked inside. My mother checked to see if I had properly brushed my teeth before the butler served me breakfast. The butler had changed the color of the same type of uniform he wore the previous day, and I was curious enough to ask if he had different colors of the same dress. Everyone laughed when I asked this. When I finished my breakfast and cleared my table, I went to join my grandfather and sat beside Star to listen to his story. My grandfather was an excellent storyteller and was also very dramatic as he told us the story of the tortoise and the hare. Star and I got chocolates for being great listeners after my grandfather was done with his story. He then took us to his room to show us our gifts. He first handed Star her gift; Star's gift was a Barbie dollhouse that she could walk inside and live there if she wanted to. It was so large that I wondered how such a gift had entered the house without my knowledge. Star planted a huge kiss on my grandfather's face and immediately began to play with her new set of Barbies.

My gift was next. My grandfather asked me to cover my eyes before he presented it. I had already started to doubt him at that point because I knew it would not be easy getting a car for me. A kid in my school who had one came from a rich family and I never knew if we were rich or not. When my grandfather finally asked me to open my eyes, I saw the largest car ever connected to a screen. The car had no roof but had doors and other features of a car. My grandfather told me it was to teach me how to ride a real car while also having fun because I would be learning through a video game. I was extremely shocked because I had not really expected such a gift. I had to run to where my parents were and I excitedly showed them the gift. That morning, my excitement could not be measured. I played with my new car all day and was so anxious to resume school on Monday so I could tell my friends. I also taught my grandfather how to swim and he learnt so fast that I promised to give him one of the stickers that was given to me by Coach Arnold.

"You should try doing the butterfly stroke, Grandpa!" I shouted as my grandfather floated on the water. He looked so relaxed that I assumed he was sleeping. Coach Arnold had once told me that if I noticed a swimmer becoming perfectly still in the water I should always scream for help because the person might need CPR. I did that as soon as I noticed that my grandfather had stopped moving in the water; my parents rushed outside and helped take him out of the water.

My grandfather did not still wake up after he was brought out of the water, and even after my dad had pressed his chest gently still nothing happened. That was my first pool scare and the universe had also not just stopped at one. My grandfather was rushed to the hospital and I had to stay at home with my sister and the butler who I found out was named Paul. I had been unable to do anything that day as I felt the worst was going to happen to my grandfather.

When it was bed time, I took the house phone and placed it by my side just in case my parents called. My mother called me few minutes after I had dozed off; I had actually assumed sleep was going to run away from me because of the situation, but that did not happen. My mother told me that my grandfather was alive but that he and my grandmother would be traveling home the next day because of his health. She also told me that since they would not be coming home that night, I was expected to look after my sister as the man of the house. I slept better that night after hearing the news that my grandfather was better; I even heard his laughter echoing in the background as my mother passed the phone over to my father for me to talk to.

My parents arrived with my grandparents the next day. I had been sleeping when they walked in and as soon as I heard our door make a sound I quickly ran out to check who it was. I saw my grandfather sitting in a wheelchair and I felt very sad; he looked tired and old, but he had not lost his smile. I ran to him when I saw him being wheeled in. My grandmother also did not look herself as she no longer looked like the prim and proper woman I encountered the first time I saw her. She looked sad and had even patted my head when I sat on my grandfather's legs. I also noticed that Paul the butler almost shed a tear when he caught a glimpse of my grandfather in his wheelchair.

We all took a shower and got ready to see my grandparents off to the airport, they were going to take a private jet. I begged my parents to let me follow my grandparents, but they refused. My grandfather apologized to me for missing out on a part of my life and begged me to forgive him. I did not understand what he was saying at that time so I just hugged him instead. My grandmother also gave me a gift; she gave me a phone number and told me to call the person whenever I needed help. Star ended up eating the paper two days after my grandparents left.

When we got to the airport, saying goodbye was the hardest thing, I saw my mother cry for the first time and my father's eyes also became teary. I was given the chance to check out my grandparents' private jet; their jet had all the fancy buttons a child like me would be interested in pressing. I also saw how my grandfather wheeled his wheelchair into the jet, and this seemed very cool to me at that time.

CHAPTER SEVEN

The news of my grandfather's death reached us a week after their departure from our house. It was a very sad day in our family as my mother was inconsolable. I felt sad but not as sad as my mother. My grandmother came back to the United States to bury her husband, but I was not allowed to go to the ceremony and my mother asked me to watch over Star instead. Everyone was dressed in black on the day my grandfather died, even the butler Paul wore black. My grandmother stayed with us at that time so we often received guests who came to pay their condolences. They did not come with gifts but with tears instead and I concluded at that time that I preferred birthdays to burials. It wasn't too long after my grandfather died that my grandmother also died. She had not been able to live alone and had become very depressed till she later fell sick.

My mother tried all her possible best to make Grandma feel better again, but nothing seemed to work. I also tried to cheer her up each time I came back from school, but that had not worked. On his part, Coach Arnold tried to help my grandmother by inviting her to come and stay with us, something he had never said to anybody. Yet, my grandmother still died despite all efforts. Her death was more painful to me because she had lived with us. I had gotten used to her grump days where she would join Coach Arnold in screaming at me if I was not swimming well. She would also argue with my mother on days like these over pointless things; arguing seemed to be her strongest power because even when she felt sick my mother was still not able to win an argument with her. My father and grandmother had also bonded during her short stay in our house; they had been able to move past the hurt they both caused each other. She had given my dad a gift by opening another gadget store for him in another location of our town. My grandmother was proud of how my father took care of my mother, Star and me when she had pushed us away. This final acceptance was one of the things that made it more difficult for any of us to move on. My grandmother's burial was very lavish and classy as this had been included in her will. She had wanted everyone to be happy during her funeral and that was what happened.

Summer came around and the sun decided to shine with full force. The swimming pool became the best place for me to hang out at every point and I sometimes pretended to be practicing for a race while most of the time I was just running away from the scorching sun. The pool provided me with a feeling no air conditioner ever did and most of the time I wished that my sister loved the swimming pool as much as I did so we could both play in it. Star was not a fan of water and her worst time of the day was always shower time. I, however, tried to convince her to like the water and I knew that I was one step closer to achieving my goal.

My dad came home one particular day and announced during dinner that we were traveling to Paris. Everyone was surprised before we all happily broke into a dance. I had never been out of the States at my age and I felt glad because I was finally spending my summer on vacation and not in my father's store. My dad had booked our tickets and we were given just three days to pack up before we left for France that summer. I was old enough to pack a bag at that time and so all my mother did was cross check what I had packed before she gave me her ready to board the plane stamp of approval.

On the day of our flight, my parents woke up late because they had been very tired from the previous day's work. I was the one who woke them up and they were very grateful for the alarm I had set. We all rushed to the airport like lunatics because we were scared of missing our flight. When we got to the airport, we were delayed a bit because the lady who was supposed to check us in did not believe we owned the first-class tickets that we had. She took one last look at our appearances and concluded that we were impostors. My dad and my sister were still dressed in their pajama tops, only the bottoms had been changed as they had both been indecisive about what shirt or T-shirt to wear. I and my mother, on the other hand, still managed to dress well despite being in a rush.

My parents felt insulted about this and even threatened to take the whole airline to court. When the mean lady realized who my grandparents were and my status as the kid swimming champion, she immediately became very humble. My mother asked the airline to remove her from her post because she had bad interpersonal skills. The flight to France was delayed because of us and we were also upgraded to the best seats in the first-class lounge. When the plane took off, I felt my heart fly into my mouth. I became very scared and clutched the arm of the seat tightly to keep myself from freaking out all the more. When my mother realized I was nervous, she gave me a pill to take and it helped calm my nerves. The flight became more bearable as we watched a movie together; Star slept through the entire journey and my mother changed her clothes into something less questionable. My father also went to change in the toilet and I could not help but wonder how he had been able to stand and walk while the plane was still in the air. It also made me imagine a lot of scenarios in my head and so I breathed a sigh of relief when he returned to his seat.

I finally managed to open my eyes when the pilot informed us that we would be touching down in Paris soon enough. At that point I finally gave up on sleep as it seemed that it was not ready to find me. I was jealous of my sister and my dad who both slept like royalty, leaving my mother and me to deal with our fear of heights.

I finally gathered the courage to look out of my window as we were about to touch down. I breathed in deeply like my mother asked me to and still got a little peck before I finally opened my eyes. I was totally captivated by the city of light; I had already done my research on Paris and I was not disappointed when I discovered it paid off. I always thought Denver was a well-lit city, but I could not believe how wrong I was because it was nothing compared to Paris. As the plane landed, I found myself ready for the adventure the city of light would provide. I was unable to believe at first that I was finally in the city of light. I blinked twice to ensure that I was not dreaming.

The baggage claim process was always an unbearable experience for my mother, there would always be something to stop her from receiving her baggage on time like other passengers. Sometimes, it would be others taking her luggage after mistaking it for theirs, other times it would be her suitcase being put on another plane to a different country. No matter how careful they were in checking her luggage, even in a separate area, my mother's bags always still went missing. She warned us all of her usual luggage problems and advised us to be patient as she always found a way to reclaim it. However, to her surprise, this time her baggage appeared alongside ours.

My mother who had already gone to the back at the time her baggage arrived with ours could not believe it when my father raised it up for her to see. She stood there for a few seconds before coming to properly inspect the luggage and make sure it was really hers and not just a bag that looked like her own.

My mother instantly fell in love with the city of Paris and her excitement was written all over her face. As I got out of the plane, I was ready for whatever adventure I would get. I had already promised Lance, my best friend, that I would send pictures and stuff to him from Paris. His mother had made him go to a swimming summer camp. This was because Lance's parents wanted him to be a professional swimmer when he grew up, and they always made him practice even when he was tired. His coach was not as nice as Coach Arnold and would always engage me in a race with Lance whenever I went to their house. He would also end up shouting at Lance whenever I won the race; he would make us race and race until we could no longer flap our hands. When I told my father, he almost stopped me from going to Lance's house and so I promised myself not to mention it again.

The streets of Paris were as busy as the streets back in Denver. The mini taxis honked their horns tirelessly as they sped through the road cussing each other out in French. I actually expected to see everyone wearing a beret, but I was surprised to see everyone dressed like normal Americans. We passed a bakery on our way to the hotel and I smelt the buttery smell of bagels and croissants, which made my stomach grumble in anticipation of dinner. I missed my mother's bakery at that point.

I started to get car sick on our way to the hotel as the hotel was a far distance from the airport. I was happy when the road finally became void of traffic and we were able to arrive at the hotel on time. My mother had asked us to pack light in anticipation of new things, for she had always enjoyed shopping. There was a time when we went to the supermarket with my mother and she made me walk the whole supermarket just because she wanted to check things out. We were even forced to ask my father for help in moving stuff out of the car because of the quantity of things we bought.

As my mother went to collect our room keys from the receptionist, I marveled at the volume of artwork that hung in the lobby. The place actually looked like a museum of arts, and I wondered at the amount of work that was put into designing the lobby. The room my mother got for us was extremely large; the chairs were so fluffy and the king-sized bed looked so inviting.

I yawned loudly and made my parents look at me strangely. My parents asked me to undress and take my bath first since they saw that I was very tired. When I got to the bathroom, I had a jaw-dropping moment. The bathroom was the largest bathroom I had ever seen and I marveled at how it was designed to take a deep bath.

My stomach grumbled again and my mother asked me to check the mini fridge, which was filled with many snacks. My mother asked me to select just a few snacks for myself and Star because she knew how much I loved eating snacks. By the time I was done eating my snacks I was already full and could not eat the food that was ordered by my parents. I climbed into bed as the plush curtains in the room gave the room a dark and mysterious feel. Soon I fell into a deep sleep due to jet lag and how tiring the flight was.

The next day, we had all rested and I became very excited to witness the beauty of Paris. My mother dressed my sister in a fancy "I Love Paris" T-shirt that I teased her about. I loved going out with Star as strangers often stopped to tell her she was a beautiful baby; there was an individual who stopped me once in the street to ask if Star could be a model for their children's cereal brand. When I informed my mother about what happened, she just laughed it off and we never got to find out if she would have allowed it at the end of the day.

My father got us a tour guide for the day, his name was Jacques. Jacques was a tall man who spoke French with so much fluency that when he spoke English he still said some things with a French accent. I liked him the moment I saw him because he made Star laugh. He was dressed in a cool jacket with trousers that looked very skinny. Star decided to take my hands as Jacques took us to our first stop—Boulevard St. Michel towards the Seine river. I could not help but marvel at how beautiful Paris really was.

My parents stopped at the blue gate of a famous bookstore called the Gibert Jeune; they rarely went to bookstores despite being lovers of books. Their busy schedules gave them no chance to read as they were either in the store or taking care of me and Star. Jacques nudged us to go ahead into the store; as we entered, I was hit in the nose by the peculiar book smell. My mother and father had separated from us as they went to a different section of the bookstore where their favourite genres were located. They were able to pick out a few books and met at the checkpoint to pay for their books; my sister and I also got some story books and coloring books. We promised to finish our books during our vacation; however, I knew I was going to spend more time in the hotel pool than with the books.

As we stepped out of the bookstore, the delicious aroma of cheese, bread, chocolate and coffee wafted out of the crowded sidewalk cafés. I wondered why everyone had not become overweight from the food that smelt so tasty.

As my parents left the bookstore, they felt more elated than they were moments before we entered. Our adventure continued and as we walked the streets of Paris; we encountered so many tourists along the way heading down the Quai des Grands Augustins. I found it difficult to pronounce a lot of French words and even began repeating any French word Jacques said. This was so I could make an A in French in my next academic session.

As the evening drew near I got to witness a very breathtaking view. I had never seen the beauty of the sun, yet I realized that the sun had a way of making things look more pretty despite the usual sunburn it gave me. The sun beat down on the sparkling river as we passed by one of the famous bridges in Paris—the Pont Neuf. It was a breathtaking sight that I quickly captured with my camera.

Our next stop was La Tour Eiffel. It took time before my mother agreed that she was not dreaming but was in fact standing next to the Eiffel Tower and could actually touch the walls of it if she wanted to.

It was not a postcard sent to her by someone but was actually very real. She had dreamt of coming to Paris as a child, but her mother always refused to take her along with them when she traveled there. She instead asked my mother to study for her exams. In fact, her short vacation without her mother was the only chance my mother had to go to a school party. It was at the school party that she met my father, so she really had no regrets. I felt scared of the thought that I was going to fall. When she noticed how fidgety I was, Star reassured me. She held my hands tightly as we moved to a better spot on the Eiffel Tower.

My mother was amazed at the impressive structure before her, and a feeling of bubbly excitement came over us. My mother told my father that she could see why most French people called American tourists tacky whenever they visited the Eiffel Tower. The tower was more than magnificent, and my mother did not care if she had become one of those tacky Americans. She even felt like she was on top of the world. Jacques pointed to some pretty interesting places that we could see from the Eiffel Tower and I was able to forget my fear of heights at some point.

Jacques took us to a spot called eternal love where we all wrote our names on a piece of paper, tucked it into a padlock, locked it and kept the key in our pockets. Jacques explained to us that not everyone who came over to the spot declared their affection for another person, and thus this practice was just a way of leaving a piece of you in Paris. Star wanted to write everybody's name on her paper and argued tirelessly with Jacques when he informed her that she was expected to write only her name on it.

After our emotional visit to the Eiffel Tower, we found our way to our next destination, which was Champ de Mars. As we walked towards the Seine, I witnessed the beautiful view of the endless field that seemed to spread before me. As we walked underneath the tower to Champ de Mars, I could not believe that I was not exhausted despite the distance we had covered.

When we got to our destination, Jacques saw a wide field packed with tourists and locals eating and reading in the sun.

My father and mother found an open spot on the grass, and we all settled down and stretched out on the lawn. I stared up at the deep blue sky and the fluffy white clouds that brushed the top of the Eiffel Tower as they floated by. My sister fell asleep immediately we settled down and I could hear her little snores as she slept. It was something I would come to miss later on.

We all took a short nap while we were seated on the ground; we did not realize how tired we were until our eyes started closing. Jacques took us to a little restaurant when we finally woke up hungry; the restaurant was Italian and was so pretty that I asked if I could be allowed to take pictures of it.

I had the most amazing dinner ever. As an appetizer, we started with a bowl of soupe à l'oignon that had about an inch of gooey, melted gruyère cheese layered over a hot, bread-filled broth. Next, we dug into a small niçoise salade topped with tuna, juicy red tomatoes and some crisp cucumbers. Finally I nibbled on a juicy chicken breast with buttery carottes fondantes on the side. For dessert, we feasted on seven different types of cheeses, from the light and creamy Camembert to the pungent Roquefort. And just when I thought I could not take anymore, the waiter lifted the lid off a platter of chocolate praline cake. I was not able to say no to cake and I did not plan on starting that day. I was very full and unable to stand up from my seat. Jacques called a taxi for us and we all dragged ourselves into it. By the time we got to our rooms, we were so tired that my parents allowed me to go to sleep without showering.

CHAPTER EIGHT

The next day, my parents went to the cathedral, which was considered a jewel of medieval gothic structure. My mother could not stop talking about how breathtaking Notre Dame was. It was surrounded by different masses of stone sculptures and my mother educated me on the significance of each sculpture when we got back home. I spent time with Star; we watched television and ate enough chocolates to our satisfaction. I also took Star to the play section of the hotel as my mother informed me to drop her off there if I was going into the pool. When I got to the play section, I saw other children there and felt more comfortable about leaving my sister there. I had expected her to make a fuss when I dropped her there, but she was more than happy and went to play with children her age.

When I got to the swimming pool section of the hotel, I was stopped by the lifeguard who was on duty.

"You cannot swim in this pool if you are under eighteen, you will have to go to the kiddies' pool," he informed me.

I looked at the kiddies' pool and knew there was no way I would go in there. The pool looked like it had no depth and I could not recall the last time I found myself in such a pool.

"I am a good swimmer," I told the lifeguard.

"That does not count, how old are you?"

"Almost eleven," I replied, trying to feel older.

"Well, eleven is not eighteen. So please find your way to the kiddies' pool." The lifeguard said this eyeing me while he blocked my path.

I did the craziest thing that day, I still consider it the funniest thing I ever did as a child. I ducked under the lifeguard's legs and dived into the pool. Having seen what I did, he shouted before he jumped in after me. I guess he chased after me because he thought I was going to drown. My competitive spirit immediately kicked in and I imagined the lifeguard being my opponent; he chased me around the pool while I enjoyed myself as I swam. The lifeguard finally stopped when he discovered that I could actually swim very well. People clapped as he got out and allowed me to continue swimming. I enjoyed the pool, especially as a pretty girl who was older than I asked me to teach her and her boyfriend how to swim. It was really a fun-filled experience for me. When my parents came back, I told them what happened before they heard it from the manager, and they advised me to listen to people who were older than I was as they knew better.

Our vacation was filled with fun as we engaged in a lot of family bonding activities. My parents went on romantic dates in the city of love and had never looked happier. My sister and I also spent a lot of fun times together as my parents allowed Jacques to take us out. Jacques took us to Disneyland in Paris; Star and I thought he had planned on taking us to a restaurant, but we were very shocked when we saw ourselves in front of Disneyland. My sister was the happiest person on Earth that day as she skipped all through the park in excitement. Immediately we entered Disneyland, she had wanted us to meet her favorite princess, but I convinced her to come on a boat trip first before going to see her princess. The boat trip was fun as I had never been on a boat before. My sister finally met her favorite princesses including Cinderella, Snow White, Sleeping Beauty, Jasmine and her absolute favorite Princess Ariel from *Little Mermaid*. I took photographs of her standing with these statutes and she was even given a makeover for the photos. I also saw characters from *Star Wars* and I even got to take some really cool pictures with Luke Skywalker and Darth Vader. We also saw a show and laughed a lot during the show. Jacques finally gave us a wonderful treat; he got us cotton candies, chocolates, pop corns and a lot of goodies. My sister was so pumped on sugar that I assumed she was never going to stop bouncing up and down. When we got home that day, Star and I narrated how blissful our day was to our parents. They were happy that we had fun, and we all planned how we were going to spend our last day in Paris before we slept.

The next day, we all went shopping for our friends. I got some really cool figurines for Lance and some chocolates and stamps for some of my other friends in school. My sister got some Barbie dolls for her friends while my mother and father also bought some gifts for their friends too and things for their store. When we returned back to the hotel in the evening, we all packed our bags before we slept that night. My parents did not make the same mistake of oversleeping and they woke up earlier than normal that day in order not to miss our flight. I woke up still sleep starved the next morning, and my mother made us march to the airport early. Jacques came by to say goodbye to us, he gave Star and me gifts, and I knew I would miss Paris. Everything had gone so smoothly, and it didn't occur to me that something bad was going to happen.

CHAPTER NINE

The last day of summer was the day death knocked on our door again and we were unable to stop it from entering. We all woke up happy that morning and there was nothing amiss as we all joked and played with each other. My father tried to convince Star to eat her peas, but she refused. It was really funny to see them argue with each other. My sister had inherited my grandmother's talent for arguing and I could see why they bonded with each other so well.

"If you do not eat your peas, I will not get you ice cream on my way back from work," my father said.

"If you do not buy me ice cream, I will tell Mother what you did with her red sweater last week," my sister countered, careful not to allow her voice within my mother's earshot.

"What are you guys saying? Star, eat your peas," my mother said as she tickled her.

My sister giggled and ate her peas, leaving my dad with his mouth wide open in shock.

"You would answer her?" my dad said, confused as to why my sister had started eating her peas when my mother had asked.

"Sure. Would you still buy me ice cream?" Star asked my father, sweetly.

"No," my dad said, grinning.

"Mother, there is something I would like to tell you," my sister said, smiling mischievously.

"Don't mind her, babe," my father said to my mother who was frying my pancakes.

"So we have a deal?" Star asked my father.

"Yes we do," my father said before lifting her up from her chair and causing her to laugh.

"We will be late if we do not get going now," my mother told my father as she placed my pancakes in front of me. She removed her apron and went to her room to fetch her bag. My sister followed her badgering my mother with a lot of questions. My sister was a very curious person, and there was no question she would not ask; there was even a time when she asked my father why his stomach was very big and she had wanted to know if he was pregnant. This statement alone convinced my father to start going to the gym. In school, her class teacher had threatened to have her start high school at three years old if my parents did not keep her curious nature in check. She was way ahead of her peers at three and could solve my math assignment with me before the summer break. My parents asked me to stop teaching her stuff since they did not want her to skip out on growth as a child. She had then shifted her attention to my mother and made it her duty to disturb her with questions at every available opportunity.

"Bye guys, see you soon," my father said and hugged us before heading outside.

"Love you guys," my mother said as she kissed us and headed outside too.

These were the last statements my parents made before

death found its way into our house. My sister insisted that she wanted to play outside when she got tired of playing indoors. I got my swimsuit, and together we both went outside.

"Let me know when you are hungry," I told her as I placed her in a box I made out of the chairs that we kept near the pool. I made sure I kept her in a place where I could see her even while I swam.

Star nodded and began playing with her dolls. I went to the pool and swam for an hour before I heard Star call my name. I had occasionally been checking on her to see if she was fine and I was glad each time I had noticed that her Barbie dolls kept her very occupied. When she called me, I immediately dashed out from the pool thinking something was wrong.

"Are you hurt?" I asked.

"No, I am not," Star said with a smile.

"Okay, so what is the problem?"

"I am hungry," Star told me.

"What would you like to eat, Princess Star?" I said, faking a British accent and bowing to her like one of those fancy princes in her princess movies.

This made Star giggle before she busted into laughter.

"I would like to eat pasta and Mother's favorite sauce," she told me after thinking long and hard.

"I can't make that, Princess Star, only Mother makes that. So please pick something else."

"I don't know," Star said sadly.

"Okay, would you like cookies and milk? I can bring enough cookies so we can watch the Cookie Monster Show as we eat our cookies," I suggested.

"Yaayh, I would love that," Star said, clapping excitedly.

I carried her and put her in one of the chairs.

"I will be right out Princess," I said, making her giggle again.

I opened the door for death the moment I went in to get cookies and milk. I hurried back outside because I disliked leaving her alone. When I got outside, I could not see my sister on the chair; I searched where she sat and I still could not find her. At that point, my heart began to beat faster than normal, and I started screaming my sister's name, hoping she would respond wherever she was.

"STAR, WHERE ARE YOU?" I shouted into the air.

As I searched, I saw a Barbie doll floating in the water. It was my sister's Barbie, and so without a second thought I jumped into the water. I saw my sister lying face down in the water, and I immediately carried her to the surface. It was obvious that she had swallowed a lot of water because she looked very pale. I tried pressing her chest gently like I had seen people do in movies, but she still did not move. I rushed to our phone line and called the ambulance before I called my parents. They freaked out and with a sense of urgency asked me to text them the address of the hospital to which the ambulance was taking my sister. I rode with my sister in the back of the ambulance with the paramedics, and for every time my sister's chest was pushed, and there was no response. I felt my heart break and I felt my head go dizzy when the paramedic started to shake her head. I did not know what the shaking of her head meant, but I knew it did not mean anything good.

"Are your parents on their way?" the female paramedic asked me.

"Yes," I replied.

What I really wanted to know was how my sister was doing and why they were no longer pushing her chest. The ambulance's tires came to a screeching halt in front of the hospital, and I saw someone rush out with a stretcher. The paramedic carried my sister and placed her on the stretcher; she looked paler and I wondered why she was losing color. She started to look like my grandmother when she died. My parents arrived at the hospital the very moment my sister was rolled inside; they met me standing outside the hospital. I didn't move despite the number of times they called my name. I eventually gave in to the darkness when the shock of what happened finally got to me. The last thing I heard before closing my eyes was my mother shouting.

"Not my son too," she screamed before I blacked out.

My sister Star died that day. When I slipped into darkness, I dreamt of Star. I dreamt of Paris, and I dreamt of holding her little hands. In my dream, Star was alive, and she gave me one of those sweet hugs that always made me happy. She told me to be fine; she also told me to take care of our parents. She wore her princess dress and told me all her princesses were in the light; as such, she wanted to meet them. She told me goodbye and waved her little finger at me for the last time.

My sister was gone, and when I woke up it was time for her funeral.

CHAPTER TEN

My sister had a special child-sized coffin for her burial. It was lined with silk with a silver handle, which was overly shined and looked like one of the fancy plates my mother had used when my grandparents first visited. Star lay in her favorite dress with the big fairy wings. My mother allowed her to wear her princess shoes. I believed my mother had allowed her to wear this because it was a very special occasion. My sister's face was pale and wrinkled like an old lady I once saw who I had been told was a hundred years old. She was this way because she had been in the water for too long. The guests that came for the burial gathered around the coffin, and the white church swelled like a whale that was about to give birth.

The priest with the curly white hair brought out his Bible as he walked towards the pulpit. I had never seen him smile at anyone, so his solemn look seemed very perfect for the occasion. He told people not to stand too close to the coffin, especially because they had no plans of resurrecting my sister. The long candles on the altar were crooked to the side; it was as if whoever made them was angry with their lengths since the short ones had been perfect.

There was a lady at my sister's funeral who cried so much that we all wondered if she was the one who killed my sister. She claimed to be my father's aunty, and she sought him out when she heard of the tragic news of my sister's passing. She tried to befriend me at the funeral, but I paid her no attention. I was in too much pain to even listen to her. The priest only allowed the family to stand beside Star, but my dad insisted some friends stand by us too. My mother stood beside her friend Mrs. Shaw. Mrs. Shaw stood beside her husband, who had never met Star, so I wondered why my father allowed him to stand with us. Lance did not come for the burial, so I stood beside my mother and father. My sister's teacher, who always said Star was curious, had come too. I also was not able to understand why she came for the funeral since Star had not really liked her. Jacque had come too, he left France and came to see Star in a coffin and I did not understand why. He should have visited when she was still alive I thought that day. I really did not understand why all these people came. We hugged briefly when the priest allowed us to. Mr. Greg also stood with us as at the funeral. I did not mind his presence as much as I minded the other people. Star smelled of cologne and coffin wood; she looked like she was sleeping and was going to wake up. I really wanted her to wake up so I prayed to God, I even prayed for a time traveling machine that would take us back in time. I never wanted Star to leave because I knew she had a wonderful life ahead of her. Still, she never woke up. Instead she remained the same.

My mother's tears trickled down from behind her black shades and trembled along her jaw like raindrops on the edge of a roof. She looked small in a black gown. She had buried three people already in just one year. She did not look okay and the only time she tried smiling was to convince me to eat.

She smiled at me when I ate my food. Her hair was tied in a black scarf and her eyes were swollen from all the crying she had been doing the day before. The doctor recommended that we took a sleeping pill and we did just that. It helped us sleep.

When my sister's coffin was lowered into the ground in the little cemetery that belonged to my grandfather, I was happy that my sister had gone to be with people she knew. I knew my grandparents would take care of my sister, so that made me happy a little. I heard the soft sounds of the brown sand and the hard sounds of the tiny roses that seemed to scratch the bright coffin polish.

The sad priest's voice was heard as he instructed everyone to repeat after him.

"We give this child into your hands, our most gracious Father, the soul of this lovely child departed. And as we give her body to the ground, we say earth to earth, ashes unto ashes, dust unto dust."

My sister was dead.

CHAPTER ELEVEN

Two months went by and the loss of my sister was not something I got over. I was not able to go to school and I always spent the whole day crying on my bed. My mother and father were not any better; in as much as they tried to be strong for me I could still tell that they were hurting as much as I did. My mother stopped going to the bakery and it took the intervention of her friends before she finally left the house. My father became equally miserable after my sister died, it was strange not to see him talk as he had always been good at talking. He walked like a ghost on a revenge mission and the only time I ever saw him smile was when he stumbled upon a video I had made of Star. In that video, she was wearing my father's shoe. She tried to make a very funny impression of him and did a very wonderful job as she also wore his shirt, which turned out to be a long flowing gown for her.

My parents also made it their duty to always check on me twice before going to bed. I once heard my mother cry beside me having thought that I was already asleep that day; she held my fingers in her hands and wept. She prayed that night as she asked God not to take me away from them; I did not agree with her and had equally prayed for God not to answer her prayers. I already started to lose belief in God at that time as I was unable to understand why He allowed my sister to die first. The priest told me that it was God's plan to take her to heaven, but I never believed him. I wondered why God would take someone so young, someone younger than I was, when I assumed death was meant only for old people.

It became seven weeks since I entered the swimming pool. Coach Arnold still came each day to try cheering me up. He told me several times that going for a swim might help make me feel better, but I knew that would not be so as nothing could make me feel better except if my sister was brought back to life. My midnight terror also started around this time, I would often have a dream where Star would be alive. She would always be wearing this white dress and would have a lot of butterflies in her hair. She would smile in the dream as she played with her Barbie doll; the same one she had been playing with on the day she died. In the dream I would often appear out of nowhere. The location of the dream was never constant as I once even found myself in Paris in the dream, and it all felt very real. Once I appeared and started walking towards my sister, she would start walking away too no matter how hard I tried to quicken my pace. She would begin to run, often like a cheetah hunting prey, and I never seemed to catch up with her. Every day I had this dream; I woke up sweating profusely and would be unable to fall back asleep again. There was, however, a particular day when the dream got worse. It was the day my mother and father decided to take me to a therapist.

As I lay on my bed that day, I did not dream of my sister at first, but later I did. I was beside a lake and just stood there looking around, I was very confused as to why my sister did not yet show up and I wondered if God had taken her out of my dreams too. In the dream, I sat down on the grass with tears rolling down my eyes, and then I heard my sister giggle. I immediately went to where the sound came from and saw that she was playing by the lake. She wore the same white dress she had worn in all my dreams and I remember how I wondered if she was never going to change her clothes.

In this particular dream, however, my sister did not run; she looked at me and smiled instead. I approached her gently with the fear that she was going to run away if I got too close, but as I moved closer I noticed she did not go anywhere. At a point it felt like she did not see me because she was so focused on her doll, but I knew she saw me as she occasionally glanced up at me with a smile.

I wished my parents could join my dream so we could all be a family again, but that never happened. I became so content with seeing my sister that I always swore never to wake up again. I did not know how I would do that, what I knew was that I no longer wanted to live in a world without my sister. My sister soon got cranky at a point and started running when I got close to her side to pet her and find out what was wrong. I followed suit and ran after her with the intention of never leaving her side until I saw her run into the lake. She jumped into it like it was and I planned on jumping in with her. However, when I got to the lake, I found the whole water bloody. My sister's white dress was floating on the surface of the pool with her Barbie doll, and she was nowhere to be found. I felt like I had watched her die again for the second time, but this time it was more horrific as she came out of the bloody water with her bloodstained white dress and told me I killed her. She repeated this many times and the next time I woke up, I found myself in a hospital bed.

My mother told me that I had been in shock when she found me and that I kept muttering, "I killed her." I saw the look of worry on my parents' faces and was glad they did not get to witness what I witnessed in the dream. I stayed in the hospital for three more days and was often given some sleeping tablets to make me sleep because I became very scared of sleeping. I was scared of seeing my sister dressed in her bloodstained white dress again and felt glad when I did not.

On the day I was to be discharged, the doctor handed my mother a note and told her to try taking me to "the place" as it would help me feel better. When I got back home, I asked my mother what the doctor meant by "the place" and how it was supposed to make me feel better since I assumed he was talking about heaven. My mother, however, told me that the doctor wanted me to see a therapist. I guess my mother was expecting my refusal because when I asked her when we were going, she looked very shocked. She proceeded to book my appointment with the doctor and also promised to come along with me. In actuality, I did not care if she came with me or not. All I wanted at that time was for the pain to pass over me and for me to get better. When night time came, my parents stayed in my room until I fell asleep. I never asked them to do so but I guess they felt that was the right thing for them to do. I woke up the moment they left and I became unable to sleep again till the drugs in my system finally took over. I did not dream again that night, but I was still restless.

The next morning, my mother woke me up very early; she helped me pick out my outfit and helped me brush my hair just like she often did when I was a child. We all ate breakfast that morning as a family, and my parents tried to make everything look very normal for me. It was as if they feared I could run away to my room and force them to cancel the appointment with the therapist.

"We are here," my mother said as she turned off the engine of the car.

I looked outside expecting to see very tall buildings with ambulances outside, but I instead saw none. My father took my hand in his and we all walked to the elevator together, hand in hand. The building had many offices in it with different colored doors too. The door to the therapist's office was multicolored and I wondered why it was painted that way.

The Ta Ta sound of my father knocking echoed in my brain and brought me back to reality.

"Hello, good morning. You must be the Jones family. I am Janet," a lady with cherry-colored lips announced at the top of her voice. Her voice was so loud that even my father flinched. She was dressed in a long green skirt, with a white top that had the words "Bad Bitch" inscribed on it. She looked like she was younger than my mother and I remember secretly praying that she should not be the one to make me feel better.

"Please have your seat and make yourselves very comfortable," Janet said as she led us to a space with matching chairs. The inside was not as loud as the outside, the whole place was painted white and every item in the room was white even to the stapler I had seen on my way in. I was scared that I could stain the room and so I tucked my hands inside my pockets for safe keeping. My father liked the idea and he also put his hands into his pockets too. Janet was the receptionist as I saw from the tag on her shirt, which must have gotten lost with the graphic sentence on her clothes. I was glad that she was not the one to make me feel better.

"Sorry about the delay, Miss June has someone with her right now, but she will be done in ten minutes," Janet told my parents and me after she dropped a teapot on our table and arranged tiny tea cups there with funny shaped biscuits. Everything was white even to the biscuits; I did not eat them because of their color. My mother poured the tea for my father and me as she claimed we needed it. I laughed when she poured so much milk in my tea for she had forgotten I did not like so much milk in my tea unlike my sister, who sometimes preferred to drink milk alone. I did not bring it to her notice but just laughed instead, I was still very sad but I laughed. My parents smiled at me, wondering what I had found to be amusing.

CHAPTER TWELVE

A tall man with sandy brown hair came out of a door while my parents and I drank our tea. He looked like he had been crying as his eyes were very red. I guess he was not expecting anybody to be in the waiting room because the moment he saw us, he frantically searched for his dark shades and put them on. As he passed by my parents, he plastered a fake smile on his face, which only gave him a funny facial expression.

"Have a lovely day," my mother called out to the man after he said hello to them on his way out.

"Miss June will see you now," Janet called out loudly to us, startling my father who spilled water on his shoes.

"I am so sorry. Do not worry; I will get that," Janet said as she picked up some paper towels to wipe the water that had spilled.

"Please follow me. I apologize once again about your shoes."

"No problem, it is fine," my father told her as she took us to a door.

Janet knocked on the door three times and it opened, it felt very magical and I wondered if her knock was like one of those secret underground knocks reserved for spies and members of the secret service. She left us immediately when the door was opened, I assumed she was going to follow us inside but instead she just told us to go in and left us alone. My parents held my hands as we moved slowly; I could feel my father's hand become sweaty and I was glad I was not the only one who felt scared. Miss June's office was not what I had been expecting; it was a spacious room that looked so homely. There was a huge fireplace with a long settee and some very colorful bean bags thrown in the corners of the room. Beautiful potted plants were arranged in some specific locations too and they gave the room a cozier look.

"Please have a seat," a woman wearing thick-rimmed glasses called out to us.

I had first taken my seat before I got to see her properly; she was a woman in her forties who had a lot of awards arranged neatly on her table. I assumed that she must have been very good in her field for her to have gotten so many awards. She had packed her hair so neatly that not even a strand jutted out, she also looked like someone who should have been on the cover of a glamour magazine with the way she sat. It was as if she was posing for the camera. As we sat down in our chairs to wait for her, she opened a file that had been sitting on her table before we walked in and began to read. She would on occasion look at the file and glance at us and I could only assume she must have been reading about us. After a few minutes she stood up from her chair and walked to where we were seated. She pulled over a bean bag and sat on it, which made her look less intimidating.

"Sarah and David, right?" Miss June said as she crossed her legs and got comfortable.

"Yes, that is us," my mother said, smiling.

"I would like you two to see Mr. Michael. He would be the best person to speak to you. I would, however, want your son to remain here," she said. "Do not worry; he is in safe hands and Mr. Michael's office is not far from here so you guys will not be far away from each other," Miss June added when she saw the fear that had crossed my mother's face.

"Would that be okay with you, Ken?" my mother asked as she kissed my forehead.

"Yes, I am good. You and Dad can go."

After confirming that I would be okay, my parents finally collected the address and phone number of the person they had been directed to. They also ensured they dropped their own cell phone number, just in case I needed to speak to them. When my parents left, it was just Miss June and I in the office. We both sat in silence for a few seconds before the strange knock was heard again on the door and Miss June smiled at me. It was a nice smile, one I had not really seen on anybody's face ever since my sister died.

"Kendrick, what's your favorite food?" Miss June asked, smiling.

I found her question strange and I hesitated before answering.

"Err... Pancakes," I said.

"Just pancakes?" Miss June asked; she looked at me as if I had said something very strange.

"With syrup," I added.

"That is much better," Miss June said, smiling at me as if I just proclaimed my love for someone. "I love mine with whipped cream, chocolate syrup and chocolate chips and maybe banana if I want to feel healthy," she added.

The banana part made me explode in laughter, I did not understand how she could still pretend that she was going to be eating something healthy after all the sugar she packed in her food. It was, however, a combination I later tried in the future.

"I heard you went to Paris too. How was the trip?" Miss June asked me.

Talking about Paris was something I had really not spoken to anyone about and I found out I could not talk for a few minutes. Miss June was breathing in and out and it felt like she had been telling me to do so I followed what she was doing. I exhaled and inhaled three times and I discovered that I was more relaxed.

"You can lie down on the chair," Miss June said when she saw how rigid I had become.

I looked at her one more time before I finally relaxed.

"Paris was great; we went to the Eiffel Tower," I said, excited at the memory of the trip. "My sister Star was there too," I added without thinking.

"Star, what a lovely name!" Miss June said.

"I named her Star," I told her proudly.

"Woow, you are wonderful at naming. If I get any pets, would you be willing to name them for me?"

This made me smile again for the second time that day.

"Can you tell me about Star?" Miss June asked with her beautiful smile still plastered on her face.

"Star is dead," I told Miss June like she was not aware of that fact.

"I know. I want to know about Star since I never got to meet her. She must have been a lovely girl."

"Yes, she was the best," I said, smiling. "She was a smart girl and very polite too, she always asked questions whenever she was curious about something. She was going to be a scientist in the future and marry a prince. She... She..." I found I could no longer talk as I had a lump in my throat from holding back the tears that threatened to fall.

"Here, have this," Miss June said, handing me a tissue shaped like Mickey Mouse.

The ridiculousness of the tissue made me laugh, especially when I didn't know what part of Mickey's body I was meant to use to clean my tears.

"Use the tail," Miss June said, smiling when she saw the look of confusion on my face.

I took Mickey's tail and used it to clean my tears, it tickled my face and I ended up laughing hysterically; Miss June also joined in the laughter. After a few minutes of laughter I surprisingly felt better and I could now talk better.

"When we went to Paris, I was very scared throughout the plane ride; my sister, on the other hand, was not scared. She slept all through the plane ride and was as excited as my mother when we finally got down from the plane. Star was a brave girl despite her age, people often marveled at the things she did because they never believed someone her age could do stuff like that. We were inseparable ever since her birth and I often taught her things I learnt from school. My mother told me that was the reason why she was so smart. Star and I were different in so many ways; she loved talking while I preferred observing people. She was very sociable and she made friends easily, this was what made her very loveable. She and my father were argued about vegetables each day as Star hated eating vegetables; I loved them and most of the time I helped her to eat them to avoid her staying too long at the dining table. I saw her fall asleep on her plate one day, when my father told her she could not watch her favorite Barbie show if she did not finish her peas. She ended up falling asleep in them and she still did not touch any of the peas. Her teacher had also planned on making her skip preschool so she could go to junior school. That was how smart she was. I was always happy she was my sister and I will forever be. But I ... killed her." I added the last part like it was a whisper.

"What do you mean by you killed her?" Miss June said, sitting up properly with a serious expression on her face.

"I left her outside to go and get cookies," I told Miss June, like saying that was enough to explain how my sister died.

"Please go on," Miss June said gently as she came to sit beside me and hold my hands.

Her hands were very cold and felt like she dipped them in ice.

"My parents left us alone that day; I wish they had not since my sister wanted to go with my mother to the bakery. They had, however, refused and told her to play with me at home, my sister did not pressure them again after finding out I was going to be at home. We both planned how we were going to spend our day after my parents left. My sister did not like swimming; in fact, she hated water and always fought my mother and father whenever it was time for her to take her bath. In contrast, I loved swimming and I began swimming even before I could walk."

Miss June looked surprised at my revelation and nudged me to continue.

"On that day, Star and I decided to go outside to play. I created a fort with the stack of pool chairs we had in our backyard and I turned it into a play pen for her. The chairs were placed at an angle where I could still keep an eye on her while I swam. I instructed her to call my name if she needed anything and I left her alone to play. Star called me when she got hungry and we joked around before she finally settled for cookies. I remember I ensured she was safe before I left her;

she was playing with one of her dolls before I even entered the kitchen. I know I did not waste time in getting the cookies and milk; it was as if I already knew something was going to happen and so I hurried. I ... got outside and saw no sign of Star... I..."

"Breathe in and out again, Ken... Yes, just like that," Miss June said as she watched me inhale and exhale. "Are you ready to go on or do you want to stop?" Miss June asked encouragingly.

I was not sure of what to do, but I knew I needed to get better so I nodded my head and continued.

"When I had searched everywhere, I decided to check the pool. I believed she could never be in the swimming pool, especially since she hated water, so I checked the pool last. When I got to the pool, I saw her doll floating in the water and that was when I knew something terrible must have happened to my sister. I jumped in the pool and I saw my baby sister looking lifeless as her body danced with the flow of the water. I quickly rushed and brought her out of the water and did CPR on her, but she did not respond. I called an ambulance and my parents, and my sister was taken to the hospital. My sister died before she even got to the hospital. It was all my fault," I added as I opened the dam of tears that had wanted to burst open.

"It was not your fault, Kendrick; you did not make your sister jump into the pool. From what you have told me, you were an amazing brother to your sister and I am sure she loved you dearly too."

"I don't think she does ... anymore," I said in between hiccups.

"Why do you say so?"

"She told me in my dream ... she said I killed her."

"That was not your sister, Ken. Sometimes our fear often becomes our worst nightmares. Because you think you killed her that is why you are having this kind of dream. Should I tell you the story of someone I loved too who passed away?"

I nodded my head because she looked like someone who was going to tell me anyway.

"I lost my father when I was just as little as you; I had no sister or brother as I was the only child. My father died when he went to the supermarket to buy me ice cream. I blamed myself for months after his death as I felt like I was responsible. I wished several times that I was the one who died that day, and sometimes I wished I had not asked for ice cream. I also completely loathed the smell, sight and taste of ice cream afterwards. I felt my mother also blamed me for my father's death and I would lock myself in my room for days without speaking to her.

I did not realize we both needed each other and after a few months passed I was glad I came around as I saw how much my mother cried each day. I noticed that she blamed herself too for my father's death and we both talked it over. I love ice cream now and I am sure my father is in a better place looking down on me; I am glad I did not let guilt weigh me down and stop me from doing the things I loved. If guilt had won, I do not think I would be where I am today and I am always grateful for the strength I had to move on.

"You cannot continue to live in guilt, Ken. The more you do the weaker you will become. Guilt does not give you the power or strength to do all the things you have always wanted to do, it also does not allow you to live your life as you should. Instead it takes more from you and leaves you in a mediocre state. Do you think your sister would be happy to see you like this?"

I froze when this question was asked because I had never really taught about how Star would feel if she saw me like that. I stared long and hard at a particular flower plant in the office, and I recalled all the fond memories I had of my sister. These memories did not make me feel sad but actually made me smile. I had been the best brother to my sister and even though I knew I still could not forgive myself for her death, I knew I was going to try my best to still make her proud.

"I do not think so," I said in reply to Miss June's question.

"Good. So I want you to do this exercise every day," Miss June said as she handed me a sheet of paper.

I collected the paper and glanced at it without really seeing anything. My eyes were still very glossy from the excess tears I shed so I dropped the paper neatly by my side instead.

"Do you know how to play *Call of Duty*?" Miss June asked.

I was so surprised that she knew what *Call of Duty* was that I just stared at her for a long time before nodding. She then took me to a section where her television was and gave me a pad to play the game with. I had not really played any game since my sister had died and was happy to play the game that day.

My parents came an hour later to take me home and were very surprised to see me playing games and laughing with Miss June. My father's eyes almost got wet again. My mother thanked Miss June a lot like she was a magician or a miracle worker, this made me giggle. My parents also fixed more appointments for me with Miss June and they all agreed I was to be homeschooled for a while before I returned to school. I was happy at that time because I was not ready to face my friends yet. Juliet gave me a lot of candy before I left her office that day and I was very excited because it felt like Halloween had come early.

CHAPTER THIRTEEN

A year had passed since Star's death and Miss June alongside my parents decided it was time for me to go back to school. I was still not confident that I was ready to face people yet, but my mother encouraged me to get prepared and even went on a back-to-school shopping trip with me. She believed it was going to lift my spirits, but it only did the opposite and made me scared. I was dressed in a simple blue shirt and jean trousers on my first day back in high school. I had skipped two grades because of my excellent sportsmanship and my outstanding academic excellence. I had also won many medals for the swimming team and I became very popular even though I was extremely shy.

On my first day back to school, my mother woke up early to make breakfast for me. She baked so many cakes, bread, croissants and pastries on this particular day that I was forced to wonder if we were having a breakfast party before I left for school.

"Good morning, Ken," my mother called out to me as soon as she heard my footsteps coming down the stairs. I always marveled at her ability to do this because her guess was always correct.

"Good morning, Mother," I said as I grabbed my seat and settled down at the dinner table.

I looked ahead and I saw that my sister's chair was no longer where it used to be. I did not know how I felt about the new development, but I knew I did not have to let that weigh me down so as not to get my mother upset.

"Where is Father?" I asked my mother who was still bringing out pastries from the oven. The entire house already smelled like mixed spices and I was starting to think something was wrong with the way she was baking. The last time I saw her bake like this at home was the day after my grandmother's funeral, she was so stressed out about her death that she become restless and ended up baking all day. I wondered why she was currently doing so.

"You know how your father is; he likes to take his time selecting his outfits like a contestant for a beauty pageant. I wonder why he actually never entered into the world of pageantry as he seems to be qualified," my mother said with a large smirk on her face. I was glad the part of my mother who loved to tease people had returned. Her constant teasing was something I had actually missed without even realizing it.

"What is your mother saying that is so funny, Ken?" my father asked as he walked down the stairs.

"She was wondering why you have not gone into the world of pageantry yet," I said before bursting into laughter at the end of my sentence.

"Did she tell you about the time I modeled for her? I know I was nineteen, I cannot remember how old she was. You know girls and how they like hiding their age..."

My mother blushed and threw a napkin at my father when she heard what he said. I almost gagged when I saw them blow kisses at each other.

"Guys please, I am still here," I said, trying to ensure they did not forget I was in their midst.

"What, Ken?" my father asked innocently.

I just rolled my eyes at him and dug into my blueberry pie.

"This is very nice, Mother," I said as I took more huge bites from the pie.

"Glad you liked it, tweaked the recipe and added a new flavor into it. I was not really sure it was going to be nice. I cannot wait to bring it out as the pie for the week to my customers," my mother said excitedly.

"Wait, how come I do not get a pie?" my father grumbled loudly.

"I only baked one, there are other pastries left for you to eat. You could also have this apple instead too," my mother said as she dropped a big apple in front of my father.

"So I only get an apple?" my father asked in an alarmed voice.

My mother just rolled her eyes and ushered me to get my bag so my father could take me to school.

"Ready to go now?" my father asked as soon as he saw me return with my bag.

"Yes," I said with a shaky voice.

"Call me if you need anything," my mother said as she held my hands tightly.

"Oh, please, you know this is not his first day in school, right?" my father said as he led me to the car.

"Drive safe, dear," my mother said as she nervously stood at the door and watched us leave.

As my father drove up to the school building, the familiar scenes came into view and I could hear my tummy rumbling in fear. I had assumed I was prepared but not anymore as I would rather have been at home learning from Mr. Joseph who had been my tutor for months now.

When I first met Mr. Joseph, I responded so poorly to every question he asked that he doubted my parents when they told him my grade. He did his best to make me a better student and he was successful by the end of the year. He wanted my parents to send me to a school for gifted children, but they had not liked the idea so much and the school was also not in the United States. Mr. Joseph also gave me some very good books he felt were going to help me in life, they were educational and very inspirational. It was the best gift I had received in a long time and I stayed up all night reading on the day he gave me the books.

"Ken, do you actually plan on leaving this car or do you want us to have your first class here?" my father said with a grin on his face.

I had forgotten myself as I had been daydreaming. I forced a smile to appear on my face so as not to show how scared I really was about starting school again. I knew if he mistakenly smelled fear again he would send me back home to be home schooled again; I tried to avoid that and return back to my normal life—well, at least pretend things were normal for my parents' sake. I grabbed the door handle as though it was a rope I was holding on to in order to avoid drowning while I watched my fingers shake slightly. I smiled at my father again and tried inhaling and exhaling just like I had been taught in therapy.

"Have a lovely first day, Son; like your mother said, call us if you cannot handle it. However, I believe you will; you are a strong, smart kid," my father shouted and drove his newly acquired Tesla away from the school driveway. I stared at the pavement for a long time before I finally took gentle steps towards the entrance of the school. I could already feel the hairs on the back of my hand stand up as I looked at the school building. Star begged to attend this school just because they had a pre-school and a high school together. She said she wanted to be close to me till I found out the other reason why she picked the school was because of their amazing playing ground. Green Spring High School was one of the best schools in our state, they produced excellent and well-mannered children and they were equally good at sports too. These were some of the many qualifications that made the school the most sought after in the whole state. Their admission process was as strict as getting into Harvard or Yale and they also accepted students based on a person's hierarchy in society.

The standard the school set never allowed for mediocrity from any of its students and every child was expected to reach their full potential. They also stood out from other schools by not limiting a child's abilities to the classrooms alone; the school had produced some of the best NBA players in the world and also some of the best chefs and artists. There were enough clubs and social activities for each pupil to participate in. The school had a large building with an equally large field that could allow for two simultaneous football matches to exist. On my first day at the school, I was very sure I was going to get lost even though I was handed a map. I was extremely poor with directions; I got lost and was unable to go for the first day of orientation. However, after a few months in the school, I became more familiar with the school environment. I knew the exit the seniors took to sneak out of the school without being caught and I even knew the extremely quiet places where I could hide and read apart from the library.

CHAPTER FOURTEEN

I dipped my hands into my pockets to ensure that my phone was still with me. It was starting to look like my security blanket and also the only thing that stopped me from running back home. My mother had convinced the principal to let me use my phone at all times just in case there was an emergency and she agreed.

The principal was a very strict woman and I was very shocked when my mother had told me I was free to call home any time I wanted. I never knew if she had agreed because I had lost my sister or because my mother had displayed some of her tears, which always moved people to show sympathy even if they did not want to.

As I walked the hallway with my new class schedule, I felt as if everyone was looking at me and no one really knew how to approach me. It felt like they must have all mocked me for letting my sister drown, their star swimmer lets his sister drown. I was so sure it would make the school paper headlines.

"You came!" a voice screamed nearby, which caused me to drop my timetable to the ground.

"I am so sorry to have startled you," Kevin said as he picked up my timetable and handed it over to me.

Kevin still looked the same to me; he and Lance were probably the only ones I talked to during my absence from school. They had both been very encouraging and had helped me during those days when I just wanted to give up, especially when the pain became unbearable. Kevin came over with his grandfather Mr. Greg on several occasions to have dinner with us, their presence in our house often made the sadness and grief much easier to bear. However, they stopped coming over as they traveled to Europe for a while and we had not really gotten to communicate because of the time difference.

"You thought I was not going to come so you can finally be a year ahead of me?" I asked teasingly.

"Ohhh pshht. Even if you decided to take two years off from school, I am sure you would still be smarter than me and even finish high school before me," Kevin said with a huge grin on his face.

"You flatter me, young warlock."

"OMG, you are still at it with these *Star Wars* references," Kevin said as he palmed his face.

"May the force be with you too," I said, adding to the mischief.

"It is good to have you back, Ken. Everyone missed you," Kevin said as we made our way to first period.

I did not believe everyone really missed me, but I was very sure Kevin had as he looked genuinely happy to see me.

"According to our schedule, we have almost the same classes this term," Kevin said with confidence.

"Wait, how did you know that?" I asked with shock clearly written all over my face.

"I collected your schedule from the school registry."

"And she handed it over to you just like that?" I became more perplexed than I was initially.

"Why do you look so shocked, Ken dearie?" Kevin said with an annoying pout.

"You could have been a stalker for all she knew and she still gave it to you just like that. Also I will kick you where the sun doesn't shine if you start with that crazy nickname again."

"She knows we are friends though; I had to show her my ID card and release a lot of personal information before she actually finally agreed to release it. So fear not, you shall not be stalked."

"Thank you for your very reassuring and kind words, Kev."

"I can't believe we start a new term with statistics," Kevin grumbled as we made our way into the class. "Is this world not filled with enough problems that we still have to come to school and solve statistical problems and weep if we never get to find the missing X in all the equations?"

"Why did I assume you would have grown to like statistics?" I asked Kevin with a grin on my face.

"Please wipe off that smile from your face, some of us are about to be tortured here."

The hallway suddenly went quiet as everyone quickly dispersed into their various classes, tardiness was not a trait that was condoned at Green Springs and Kevin and I were forced to hasten our steps by the school monitor who I still liked to believe had a crush on Kevin.

My talk with Kevin had completely distracted me and I did not really pay attention to the fact that we were about to enter my old classroom, a place I had not set my foot in since I lost Star; I was still not sure of the reception I was going to receive yet and I hoped to delay the inevitable. Kevin, however, had other plans as he opened the door with a loud bang. I mentally rolled my eyes in my head; I had almost forgotten how dramatic Kevin was. He was definitely an attention grabber and I started regretting not coming into class on my own.

"Mr. Jones, it is nice to have you back in my class again," said Mrs. Sheen, our statistics teacher, as she smiled and ticked off my name from the register. "Kevin, once you break down my class door, just remember you will be fixing it all by yourself," she continued, eyeing Kevin as he walked in. I did not really realize how much I had missed most of my teachers, I was not a teacher's pet but most of them just liked me because I was very well behaved and smart. I walked closely behind Kevin as he went for his chair, some of my friends smiled at me when I walked by while others seemed confused about what facial expression to give. As I got to my permanent seat of residence, a chair and table that had always been beside Kevin's, I was shocked at what I saw. My chair was now occupied by a girl with large green eyes; the eyes were the first thing I noticed about her. Her eyes reminded me of Superman's kryptonite as it glowed brightly. She had a smile on her face as if she was finally getting her long-awaited wish. She looked extremely pretty and had very long, curly, jet-black hair, which was tied into a messy bun on the top of her hair. I had never seen her before, so I was sure she was one of the new students Kevin had constantly talked about. What Kevin, however, failed to tell me was that she was occupying my space and I would have to find another place to sit.

"Oh shit, I forgot to mention her, right?" Kevin said, looking scared.

"It is fine, you probably forgot even though you remembered every dress Mrs. Sheen wore for a whole month. I am starting to think you have a crush on that woman," I replied teasingly.

"You know the only reason I remember that is because her clothes are the only things I see when she talks," Kevin said, shocked at my assumption.

"Keep lying to yourself," I said to him, winking continuously.

"Why are you two not in your seats yet?" Mrs. Sheen asked. "What is Kevin doing again this time?" she asked as she looked at him pointedly.

"What! Nothing. That woman hates me," Kevin murmured under his breath.

"I didn't get you, Kevin. Maybe you would like to come to the front of the class and let us know what it is you would like to say to me."

"It is nothing, ma'am. He was letting me know about the new seating arrangements," I said, trying to save Kevin from being kicked out of class, even though that would be something he would have really enjoyed.

"That is true. I would need to make a new arrangement for a new chair and table to be brought in for Cindy," Mrs. Sheen said as she looked around. "In the meantime, you can have my seat," she said and smiled.

Kevin and I looked at her in shock, I expected her to actually offer me her own chair and I found it quite strange that she would have asked that. I was not sure if she was doing it out of pity or because I was her best student.

"I think she must be in love with you," Kevin said while making kissing noises in my ears. I was tempted to slap him off the planet at that time.

"I will manage with Kevin for today, ma'am," I said to Mrs. Sheen.

"Are you sure? You know Kevin can be quite distracting," Mrs. Sheen said like Kevin was not in the room.

"Yes, I am sure. Thank you."

"That woman keeps hurting my feelings," Kevin said as we made our way back to his seat. I was larger and taller than Kevin already so sitting with him was not as comfortable as I imagined it to be. I was, however, able to survive his constant sighing as Mrs. Sheen explained the topic for the day. I also noticed that the new girl glanced in our direction a few times. I hoped she did not feel too bad about taking my chair; I had already expected them to have taken it away since I was absent for more than an entire school year.

Time flew by quickly and Kevin happened to be in almost all my classes. I started to believe he must have picked his classes after seeing my schedule because there were some classes I knew he had no interest in but still took. I was certain when I saw him in the culinary class; I knew how much Kevin hated cooking and I almost wept when he was given an equally unserious cook as a partner. I knew my culinary class just signed up for premium drama. His constant chit chat also took my mind off a lot of things and when it was time to eat, I settled in perfectly with my old friends at that table.

Kevin made everything very easy for me; I had assumed it was going to be very weird, but the reverse was the case. I also saw some new faces at the table that I was not familiar with and later found out that they were the two new amazing football stars that we now had in our school. Their father was a celebrity who had wanted them to play football professionally. For that reason they had picked Green Springs. The table I sat at consisted of some of the best sport players Green Springs had; Kevin, James and Paul were the school's top basketball players. We also had me as the school's best swimmer; I was secretly surprised no one had taken the title yet. We had two amazing soccer players, golf players and probably every sport you could ever think of. Unlike every other school in the state, ours had a sports team that was like a family, there was never any rift between any sport and all of our coaches often went on trips together. It was one of the few things I loved about our school.

Everyone was glad I came back and no one acted weird around me, the conversation flowed well as everyone talked about where they went for the summer. They also exchanged funny and embarrassing stories that almost made me choke on my lunch. I did not travel during the summer so I was glad I was not being forced to talk; besides, Kevin's story almost took the entire break time.

CHAPTER FIFTEEN

When lunch was over, I knew it was time to face my fears and visit the school's swimming team coach. He was also one of the few teachers that stayed in touch with me during my absence in school and when I told him I was no longer going to swim again, he was devastated. He asked me not to give up on my passion and encouraged me daily. He also got in touch with Coach Arnold who was my personal coach; together they tried their possible best to get me back into the pool again. Coach Arnold finally succeeded as I started swimming again during summer, the heat might have been a contributing factor as it was so unbearable that even staying in the air conditioned room wasn't enough.

Coach Arnold tried to help me get over my fear of swimming again, but none of his techniques had worked. He was on the verge of giving up that day until he found me swimming in the pool. I still do not know what had come over me on that day. I had woken up and just changed into my swimming gear before jumping into the water. When my mother saw me, she assumed that perhaps I was trying to kill myself. However, she saw me flap my hands in the water and that kept her mind at rest. When I finished swimming that day, I came out to behold a teary audience in front of me. They all looked so proud of me and Coach Arnold even gave me his once in a blue moon type of smile. When my coach in school heard this, he was very happy and had me make a promise to see him the first day I came to school. Now I had to fulfill that promise. Kevin tried to accompany me to the office, but I told him that I knew he was trying to babysit me. He eventually agreed to leave me alone and go for his basketball practice when I threatened to tell everybody in school about an embarrassing secret of his.

The swimming pool was at the extreme end of the school, it was a standard Olympic-sized swimming pool and I heard the school had to take out huge loans before they were able to construct it. The largeness of the pool was also what made swimming in my school a very popular and important sport as people from other schools and other countries often came to host their swimming competitions in my school. There was a particular swimming event that pulled so many crowds that the swimming area was packed and filled with reporters. That day was very important to me as I swam against some boys from Crenshaw High; they had held the state championship for ten consecutive years and Green Springs always came in second or third whenever they faced them. However, on that particular day I threw away my pre-competition jitters after hearing them make fun of our school in the locker room. Some of them even joked about not going for practice because they were so sure they were going to beat us hands down. When it was time for the competition, I actually saw one of them flirt relentlessly with a girl from a grade above me.

Their lackadaisical attitude was one of the driving forces for me and I made winning my priority. When they saw that it was I who was representing Green Springs, they snickered among themselves and their best swimmer even promised to give me a head start so I would not lose too badly. His generosity, however, cost them his title as I not only beat their best swimmer, I equally challenged each of their swimmers to a race and won all of them without breaking a sweat or breathing as heavily as they did. That day, I won first place for my school and I became very popular among swimming teams from other schools. They were happy that someone had finally put those pompous jerks in their place. The principal was also so proud of me for making our school win the title of the state championship and she gave me a huge medal from the school and even put my picture up on the wall of fame.

As I got to the pool, I saw a lot of students who came to practice for the swimming class. I hurriedly made a sharp bend to the left to avoid being seen by any of the lifeguards that were always stationed by the pool.

"Come in," Coach Jeff said.

I carefully opened the door and walked into his office. His office was always a sanctuary to me and a lot of guys on the swim team. It was a spacious room that had a great deal of trophies and medals hung in a large show glass. There were different paintings of various successful swimming athletes on the wall of his office; frames containing pictures of when he won awards during his time were also hung on the wall. My favorite picture was a picture of all of us in the swim team. It had been enlarged and placed in the center of the room; in the picture, we had all gone for pizza to celebrate a particular win and some of us were photographed with our mouths full.

"Kendrick Jones! You have finally graced my office. I was already thinking I was going to have one of the boys try to kidnap you," Coach Jeff said as he came around to give me a bear hug. He was a very muscular man and although he was now in his late fifties he was still an excellent swimmer and was in a very great shape. On the day I met him, I expected him to be a very scary person because of his muscles and his height; however, he was the opposite because he showed emotions when he saw me swim, he had also hugged me when I completed fifteen swimming laps under three seconds. I felt his muscles were going to crush me on that particular day. This was also one of the attributes that made him different from Coach Arnold; Coach Arnold was not muscular and had a smallish frame. He also never gave hugs and he rarely smiled except on extremely special occasions. He and Coach Jeff later realized that they had both competed together in the past and were happy to train me together.

"Things have honestly not been the same without you, everyone on the team has missed you and we are all glad to have you back on the team. Okay, let me not speak for them yet, but I am sure I have missed you so much. It is good to have you back, my boy," Coach Jeff said happily.

I was really not sure about joining the team again and just wanted to watch from the sidelines. However, as I listened to Coach Jeff's talk, I knew there was no way he would agree to me not swimming.

"So we should expect you at practice tomorrow, right?" he asked with his *I will not be taking no for an answer* voice.

"Yes sir, you will."

"Good, you should head out now so you do not miss your next class."

"Thank you so much, sir, for your help." I was extremely grateful for all the times he had checked up on me.

"Don't thank me; I am the best coach in the world for a reason. Don't tell Arnold I said that," Coach Jeff said almost in a whisper.

I laughed as I found my way to the basketball court; I knew Kevin was going to go late to class if I did not drag him out of the court. Basketball to Kevin was like football to me, it was something I did with so much ease. Kevin planned to be a professional basketball player and his parents had vehemently refused. This was one of the reasons why he chose to stay with Mr. Greg instead of his parents. They lived in England and they initially were very reluctant to send Kevin to America to stay with his grandfather, but when they heard of the close proximity between Green Springs and Mr. Greg's house they immediately agreed. Kevin's parents were professors and their dream was for Kevin to follow in their footsteps.

"Oh no, give me one more minute," Kevin called out as soon as he saw me.

"Let us go now, unless you want us to be late."

Kevin was the only one in the court as most of his teammates had gone back to class.

"Kevin, I hope you realize we are literally the only ones here."

"Don't forget Coach," Kevin shouted back.

"Coach does not have a class that he needs to pass."

"Heard you, Mother, but let me take a shower first before we go," Kevin shouted.

I was forced to roll my eyes at him for the tenth time that day.

The remaining classes passed by quickly and soon it was time to go home. I hitched a ride with Kevin's driver who dropped me off at the bakery. As if she was expecting us, my mother handed Kevin a take home pastry basket.

"How are you?" my mother asked as she looked at me with worried eyes. "I hope school was not too much for you today."

"I am fine, Mother, and if things had been too much I would have definitely called you. I actually felt like I had not taken a break with the way Kevin still chattered nonstop."

"Now I am glad I gave that boy that pastry basket. He really earned it," my mother said while laughing as she opened the door of the pastry shop for me.

I made myself useful when I got inside by helping out at the cash register. After about an hour my mother approached me with a sad look on her face. I was very scared something bad had happened when I saw her expression.

"Mother, what is wrong?" I asked with a panicked look on my face.

"There is a client coming in to make enquiries about wedding cakes and she also wants to do some cake tasting. I know I was meant to go home with you, but I can't do that right now," my mother said, looking very sad.

Relief washed over me as I had feared the worst.

"It is fine; I can stay at home alone."

"Are you sure?" my mother asked.

"I am very sure, Mother."

"Okay, if you say so. I could have James drop you off at home."

"No problem."

"I will be home soon. Call me if you need anything," my mother said to my retreating figure.

I was actually happy I was going home that early, I needed time to think about my first day at school. It was an exercise Miss June had recommended I do on my first day. I was also glad that the day was not as bad as I had predicted it to be; I had expected I'd have to hide in the bathroom stalls, but I was glad I didn't even shed a tear all day. I even got to laugh at my friends' jokes, something I had really missed.

CHAPTER SIXTEEN

When I got home, I tried to read a book after doing the mental exercise I had been given by Miss. June. I fell asleep even when falling asleep had started to look like an impossible task for me.

I was startled when the front doorbell rang. I looked towards it wondering who was at the door. My parents were not home and I hardly ever spoke to anyone when I was at home, I always considered it my quiet time.

I walked over to the door, grateful that my parents had decided to get CCTV cameras. I got to where the monitor was to check who it was as I knew my parents had the keys and so really had no reason to press the bell. I looked at the monitor and saw Kevin with a huge bag of chips. It was as if he knew I was going to be checking the monitor because he dangled the bag of chips, which I could now see was open, in front of the camera. I next saw Lance, Tee and two of our other mutual friends also holding something up to the camera. I rolled my eyes as I got to the door.

"Hey amigos, what brings all of you here to my doorstep?" I said, using the cliché word I knew they all hated so much.

"Please never say that again," Lance said as he pulled me in for a bro hug.

"You guys look like you are about to kiss," Kevin said with a mouthful of chips.

"We brought you your favorite type of strawberry cheesecake and some chips, which we can see are already being eaten by this foodie to celebrate your first day of school," Becky, Tee and Paul said simultaneously as if it was something they had rehearsed a lot of times.

"Weird much," Kevin said as they all make their way inside my house.

I found my smile reaching my eyes as Becky, Tee and Paul argued and followed Kevin inside my house. I had missed them greatly and was actually glad they had come around. Becky, who was named after his grandmother, was our school's best soccer player; one of his greatest pet peeves was people calling him Becky. I still always used to taunt him with it despite his hating it. He had always claimed that he was given the name Becky because his parents hated him and we all knew that was not even close to being the truth. His parents were both our family doctors and they were extremely amazing people, they loved Becky to pieces since he was their only son and they often loved showing us embarrassing pictures of him as a toddler. Becky told us on several occasions that he was going to elope with his girlfriend and go somewhere his parents would never find him to get married.

His fear was that they were going to end up playing his baby pictures on a screen at his wedding. His parents had assumed he was a girl and his mother had not bothered to get a scan while she was pregnant despite being a doctor. She decided to go with her instincts and her instinct told her that she was going to have a girl. So with that assumption, she had gone with the flow and had shopped for baby things. She had also decided on a name for him and named him after her mother, who was named Becky. Becky's mother claimed to have been very shocked when she discovered she was not giving birth to a girl but to a boy. Everyone had laughed at the theatre that day and Becky claimed that it was then his life became a joke to his parents. Becky's mother did not want to disappoint her own mother so the name had stayed and Becky was forced to wear so many cute pink dresses as a child. We all knew he initially joined the soccer team to feel more manly and overcome the so-called stigma he felt his name brought. He trained so hard that he became one of the best soccer players. With that, people stopped laughing at his name and rather respected him for his achievement on the pitch. He was also nicknamed the lion; thus, people hardly called him Becky except if they were in his class or were very close friends of his.

Tee, on the other hand, was like the Bill Gates among my group of friends. He was a professional golf player and had traveled the world over to play golf. He was mentored by Tiger Woods as a child and this made him the best golf player at his age. His parents were extremely wealthy people who had oil reserves in various countries of Africa and around the world. Tee lived in a mansion with so many servants that he sometimes was not allowed to brush his teeth himself. His parents were hardly ever home so he was a regular visitor to my house while Star was still alive. They had both been best buddies as he often brought a lot of goodies and teddy bears for Star, he also taught her how to play golf and had bought her a mini set, which she could fit in her room. He had been devastated when he heard of her death and I was unable to talk to him because I had felt he was going to blame me for letting my sister drown. I did not realize Tee had also been badly affected by my sister's death until I overheard my parents talk about it. I reached out to him shortly after and we had been able to talk things over the phone; it had also been very refreshing to hear him say that it was not my fault. We exchanged fond memories with each other and laughed and cried so much over the phone. Tee was also not one of those rich spoilt kids. He was so humble that most people he met would never know he was rich until they heard about who his parents were. He was also the one who started the golf team at Green Springs and had also volunteered as a coach before one was eventually hired.

Paul was Kevin's cousin who was transferred from his previous school when his parents heard of the excellence of Green Springs. They believed Paul needed some kind of transformation and Kevin's parents had to put in a word for them at the school before Paul was finally sent down here. He was, however, not staying with Mr. Greg as Kevin's parents had not wanted to stress the old man and they had instead made him stay with a business partner of theirs. The people Paul's parents asked him to stay with were very strict people and Paul always made up excuses for why he had to sleep over at Kevin's house before he could be granted any type of freedom. Paul was also a very good basketball player like his cousin and they always enjoyed playing one on one with each other. They were polar opposites as Paul hardly talked unless he was with friends while Kevin talked always. It was one of the things that helped me figure out why his parents had transferred him down to Green Springs. I had never bothered about asking Paul about this because I was not a nosy type. I was sure if I had asked Kevin I would have definitely gotten the truth out of him without much stress.

"Did you guys remodel your kitchen?" Tee asked as

he walked inside the kitchen. They were all so familiar with where everything was in my house that they no longer needed any form of guidance.

"Why do you ask?"

"The wallpaper looks different and I have also been unable to find my favorite plate," Tee grumbled like a girl.

"You have a favorite plate in another person's house, Tee? You are ever so bold," Becky said, smirking.

"Please, like I did not see you fill my fridge with bottles of water labeled with your girly name tags the last time you came over," Tee said teasingly.

"That was only because you guys did not have water the last time I came around. I mean a house as big as yours should have its own branded bottled water," Becky fired back.

"Oh please, that was one time and you came back the next time with a carton of water. I would like you to know that your water served a very good purpose in my house," Tee said as he winked at Becky.

"Did you use it to win over a girl?" Kevin asked, suddenly interested in the conversation as he abandoned his bag of chips on the table.

"Does everything really have to revolve around girls with you?" Lance asked while grabbing the bag of chips and eating.

"I would just like to ask why Tee and Paul are already demolishing the cake that they supposedly brought for me," I said and stared at the two guilty culprits.

"Hey, don't look at me that way. I was going to divide it and serve everybody until I discovered that my plate had gone missing," Tee said, trying to justify his actions.

"I just like cakes. Sorry," Paul said like it was no big deal.

"Speaking of girls—" Kevin tried to say before he was rudely interrupted by Becky.

"I don't think anyone was speaking of any girl, Kevin, so don't try to be smart here," Becky said.

"Well, I am sure you all would be very interested in this particular story I am about to give you," Kevin said with his eyebrows raised in a funny way.

"Is raising your eyebrows part of it? Because if it is not, I would suggest you let them return back to normal," Paul said with a pointed look.

"The story is about Ken and his soon-to-be girlfriend," Kevin said excitedly.

"Drumroll please!" Becky shouted.

"You surprise me, Ken. Your first day after a long time and you already almost have a girlfriend," Lance said as he patted my back.

"Please do not tell me you believe this guy?" I looked around at my group of friends and all of them seemed to have actually believed Kevin.

"Spill!" Paul shouted in Kevin's ears, making him trip and fall backwards.

"There is nothing to spill, guys, please ignore Kevin," I said as I tried to get their attention.

"So there is this girl named Cindy, who I am sure you all know by now—well, apart from Lance."

"What, you mean that Cindy Cindy?" Tee cut in excitedly.

"Yes it is her, so please calm down," Kevin said in annoyance. "So I caught her staring at Ken all through all of our classes today," he announced.

"Trust me when I say Kevin is literally exaggerating right now," I cried out to my friends who still looked like they had no interest in ever listening to me.

"Where does the soon-to-be girlfriend part come in

though?' Lance asked like I had not asked them to stop listening to crazy Kevin.

"Well, if Ken plays his cards right, that statement can manifest itself. Trust me; if you know who this girl is you will know why I am taking her staring at Ken as a big deal," Kevin said, addressing Lance directly so he could understand the situation properly.

"True, though I always assumed she was never going to like any guy in our school or she had a boyfriend in another school," Tess chipped in.

"Well, she does not, and we now know she is interested in Ken."

"So what is the plan now?" Becky asked.

"Hello guys, I am still here and there is no plan," I shouted.

"Could you excuse us for a moment? Let us help you brainstorm," Kevin suggested.

"Please tell me this guy is not serious? You really want to kick me out of my own house?"

"Well, either you keep quiet or you leave," Kevin finally said in annoyance.

I decided to keep quiet and watched my crazy friends set up a meeting with Cindy for me. I was unable to believe that Lance actively participated in the discussion as he rarely tolerated any of Kevin's plans. They openly talked about me like I was not in the room and I was only allowed to say yes and no whenever I felt their plans were over the top. I, however, said no continuously because I was too shocked that they were trying to set me up with a girl despite the fact that it was my first day in school after a long time. Kevin suggested that I should deliberately bump into her so I could get her number that way. Paul asked me to be direct and just ask her out if I liked her and Lance and Becky offered their suggestions with mouths filled with cake. They also eventually finished my cake without allowing me to taste it.

"You guys have not really asked the main question here," I said, interrupting their meeting.

"And what would that be?" Kevin asked as he eyed me and the empty cake box simultaneously.

"You guys never asked if I even like this girl."

"Do you not like her?" they all chorused back at me.

"Well, I do not know yet. I am not really sure," I said, stuttering.

"That settles it, tomorrow you ask her out," Kevin instructed like he was my father.

"Now that we have that settled, what movie are we seeing?" Becky asked.

"Does he still have that home theater?" Paul asked.

"Sure, I also brought my mini speakers the last time I was here; all that was left was for me to connect it," said Kevin.

"You know how to connect those systems?" Lance asked in a shocked voice.

"I can do manly things, please," Kevin answered in annoyance.

"How is that manly in any way?" Lance questioned curiously.

"OMG, I left something outside," Tee screamed suddenly in his high-pitched voice.

"What is it?" I asked.

"My puppy," he said as he ran outside to get it.

"When did you get a puppy?" I asked, shocked that his parents had allowed him to get one.

"During the summer," he said as he grabbed a dog basket from his car. "Ta da!" Tee said as he showed us his puppy. It was a German shepherd that licked all our shoes when we allowed him in.

"I can't believe you forgot you had a dog," Lance said, alarmed at Tee's forgetfulness.

"At least I was not the one who ended up finishing a cake meant for someone else," Tee said in attack.

Soon enough everyone was arguing about who finished the cake and I knew I had no choice but to let everything play out on its own. I knew that interfering with my friends' arguments was going to do more harm than good for me. Instead, I settled on the sofa and began playing with Tee's dog instead. I had always wanted a dog but my father wanted me to be responsible before he got me one. I was, however, not sure if this was the right time for me to bring up the subject of getting a dog. After a couple of minutes went by, my friends were still not close to agreeing or concluding their argument, and I knew I had to intervene before my parents came in and assumed we were all fighting.

"We could watch *Barbie and the Twelve Dancing Princesses* if this argument is prolonged," I screamed as I stood on the chair.

"Tell me he's joking," Lance asked with a shocked face.

"I don't think he is," Kevin said as he looked at me.

"Race to my room!" I ordered and everyone immediately ran to my room.

"Your room looks amazing," Paul said in awe as he gazed around my room. My room was the one thing I prided myself on because I spent the majority of my time there, especially after my sister died. It was my own personal sanctuary and I'd had it redecorated twice over the past few years.

My room was painted grey, and above my bed, I had a huge mural painting of a butterfly. The painting glowed in the dark whenever the lights were off. It took my father a three-hour drive to get the painting when it was finally shipped from Paris. It officially became my most favorite possession at that time. My bed looked more like a hundred pillows glued together than an actual bed, it was extremely huge and touched each corner of the walls in my room. Tiny stars and some large moons were also painted on the ceiling, depicting how the galaxy would look if one ever used a telescope to check it out.

I had a brown bookcase in a particular corner with different genres of books. I arranged my medals and trophies in a particular corner too, next to my music player. I also had a lot of motivational quotes inscribed on the wall; I asked for this when my sister died because I felt that my room was too bare. Reading them every day also proved to be more helpful than I had ever imagined and I became very happy I made the decision to have those words on my wall. My favorite inspirational quote was, "Never give up." It had quickly become my daily mantra as I tried each day to remain positive. My desk was next to my bookshelf, it was a simple grey mahogany wooden desk with a very funny grey chair, and three white bean bags were thrown in specific locations. My chair was funny because it often made a squeaky sound whenever someone sat on it. The squeaky sound was always hilarious as no one ever expected such a wonderful chair to make such a noise; it always startled my friends.

My wardrobe was on the extreme end of the wall, it was a built-in wardrobe with so many sections in it. The carpenter who worked on it wondered why someone my age would be using such a large wardrobe, but he did the job well, especially when he realized how much was involved. I decided to use my large wardrobe as storage space. There was a particular section that contained my clothes, which were all arranged by color and season. There was also another section where all my shoes were lined up by their sizes. The last section of my wardrobe was a storage unit. I was not able to let go of some of the things my sister owned and I had begged my mother to let us keep them, though she initially disagreed because of space. However, when she heard about my wardrobe idea she allowed me to keep some boxes of some of my sister's favorite things. That was how Kevin knew that I had possession of the *Barbie and the Twelve Dancing Princesses* movie; he was actually the only one who knew what was hidden behind the wardrobe door.

"So what are we going to watch?" Lance asked.

"*Terminator Two*," Becky suggested.

"*Terminator One*," Kevin said.

"Any *Terminator*," I said as I braced myself for another round of arguments.

"Let us take a vote," Lance suggested to the group. "There are five of us here so it should not be hard." Everyone agreed to it.

"All in favor of *Terminator One*, raise your hands please."

Kevin was the only one who raised his hands.

"All in favor of *Terminator Two*, please raise your hands." This time, it was only Becky who had his hands raised.

"I need to know why I am yet to see the hands of Ken and Tee," Lance said as he looked at me and Tee like we were criminals.

"We actually are on the fence and we would go with anyone, seems like you are going to be the tie breaker," Tee said to Lance.

"You guys are doing this again," Lance said, grumbling. "Okay, this is what we are going to do; we will allow the puppy to pick," he said in his *I just got a wonderful idea* voice.

"Tell me this is another joke?" Tee asked rhetorically. We were all aware that Lance hardly joked and was thus serious. Soon enough we found ourselves arranging a set of DVDs in front of a puppy that had earlier on been forgotten in the car. The puppy eventually touched *Terminator One* with his paw and was ready to touch the second DVD when Kevin yanked it off the floor and declared himself the winner. That day was full of fun as we watched all the *Terminators*. All my friends stayed till my parents returned and we all had dinner together before everyone was dropped off at their own houses by my father. Except for Tee anyway as he had his own personal driver who carried him everywhere. My parents were very happy when they came home to see me with my friends. I slept like a newborn baby that night.

CHAPTER SEVENTEEN

A few weeks passed and I had already started living life as a normal teenager again. My friends were still constantly teasing me about Cindy. I was also aware of the sudden feelings I started to have for her. We had met once when I bumped into her deliberately as Kevin had suggested. I just stood and looked at her. She stared at me for a long time waiting for me to talk, but I had done nothing of the sort; instead, I just remained mute. She blushed when I just said hi before leaving her alone. As I stared at her long black hair in class, I tried my best not to allow the smell of her perfume disturb me. I was already losing concentration as it was.

"Mr. Ken," the science teacher called out to me.

"Yes sir," I said, snapping back into reality.

"Please, where is your mind today?" he asked as he gave me a pointed gaze. It was a very scary one and I immediately focused on what he had been saying.

"So Miss Cindy, your partner is Ken. Your reports should be due next week and my office door is open just in case you have any questions," the science teacher said.

I was so shocked that I assumed I had misheard the science teacher. Cindy, however, made me realize it was not a dream as she walked up to me and gave me her number. I also asked her to come to my house so we could do the project together and promised to make her a meal when she arrived. I attributed my newfound boldness to Kevin and I knew he would flip out once he heard about Cindy coming over.

On that day, classes flew by as I was very eager to go home. I told my parents I was having a guest over as I got the house key from them, but I didn't tell them the sex of the person. I was very sure they assumed it was Kevin. Kevin also tormented me as I had expected; he teased me all the way home and threatened to post it on the school Twitter page if I eventually decided not to tell him how it went.

As I arrived home I ran through the door and went straight to my room. In my room, I headed straight into the shower to wash whatever dirt I must have acquired off my body. Once I had showered and dried my body, I hurriedly looked through my choice of clothes and groaned mentally at what I saw before me. I just had casual clothes with no idea on what I was supposed to wear for a study date. Well, it was not really a date, but I kind of just wanted to look nice so as to make a good first impression and probably get the chance to finally ask her out like my friends wanted me to do. When I glanced at my collection of clothes, I was forced to ponder on a bitter truth—if she was really interested in me I was sure she must have heard rumors about my sister and must have lost any interest in dating a very suicidal and depressed guy. I decided to go for a more laid back look as I grabbed a very big baggy T-shirt. That T-shirt was ordered by my father for himself but was eventually given to me when he found out that they had delivered the wrong color to him. I also picked out one of my favorite pairs of shorts to wear along with the shirt. As I was about to put on my shirt, I saw a message alert on my phone. My heart skipped with so many beats of fear as thoughts of Cindy cancelling the meeting raced through my mind. The message was, however, from my father who asked me to cook for myself since he and my mother were going to be late in returning.

I decided to make one of the fastest and easiest meals I knew how to cook—spaghetti and meatballs. It was not my favorite food but it was something I had learnt to cook easily. I boiled the spaghetti and left it to simmer as I gave more attention to the sauce I was making. It really did not take me a very long time to prepare and get dinner cooked. I was just about to leave the food in the microwave so it could retain its heat when I heard a knock on our door. My heart skipped a beat as I found my hands shaking vehemently; I soon summoned the courage to walk towards the door and decided to stand there behind it for a few seconds to gain my composure before opening it.

I looked through the monitor just to be sure it was her and not one of the boys. When I looked, I saw her playing with the lucky charm on her bag as her eyes scanned her environment. Cindy was a very slim girl with an amazing eye color, which looked like it should be on the cover of *Vogue* magazine. She did not look like most girls in our school and walked with so much grace and poise; her smile was always very warm and she always looked like an angel whenever she did so. The day I saw her sad, I felt very tempted to find out who or what had made her sad and I wished we had been really good friends at that time so I could have helped cheer her up. Another loud knock brought me back to the present as I realized I had been staring at Cindy through the monitor and had been keeping her waiting. I wondered why most of my reasoning flowed out the gate whenever she was around and I could only hope I was not trying to start something I could not finish.

I rushed to open the door for Cindy and we finally bumped heads together just like Kevin had planned. However, this time, I could have died from embarrassment as our heads collided with each other.

"I am so sorry about this," I said as I handed over a pack of frozen peas to the girl I was supposed to ask out.

"What? Sorry? You don't have to be sorry," Cindy said, smiling at me.

"I just get clumsy at times," I said, trying to justify my reason for bumping into a beautiful girl like her.

"It is fine and you have a beautiful home," she said as she looked around our living room.

"Thank you," I said, suddenly tongue tied.

"Your house smells nice, too, and from the apron you are wearing I am sure you have been cooking?" Cindy asked as she smiled at the little cute pink apron I was wearing, which belonged to my mother.

"I think I am set to embarrass myself today," I muttered to myself as I prepared to rush inside the kitchen.

"Do you want to eat now or after we start on the project?" I asked Cindy who was admiring some of the paintings hung on the wall.

"I would love to eat now, if that is okay with you," she said shyly as she took her chair.

"Oh yes, I would love to eat now, I didn't really get to eat at the cafeteria today due to swimming practice. Just take a seat and I will dish this up," I told her as I gestured to the chair at the table. I do not really know why I rambled so much in her presence. She walked over to the chair and sat herself down gracefully; I couldn't help but stop and stare at how beautiful she really was.

"So where are your father and mother?" she asked.

"They are at work and they will not be back until later," I told her as I busied myself with getting the plates out and picking my grandmother's fine china before dishing out our food and bringing it over to the table. Finally remembering to offer her a drink, I asked her what she would like.

"Just a diet Coke or anything with less sugar if you have it at home." She smiled at me then scooped a forkful of food before slowly taking it into her mouth, smiling happily as she did so.

"God, this is very good," she said as she ate the food, and I smiled widely before getting up to make us some drinks. My nerves slowly evaporated, which I was thankful for. I did not really want our entire evening to be stiff and awkward because of me. I knew I would never live it down if it was and my friends wouldn't let me have any peace. We ate the rest of the dinner in silence and after we finished Cindy helped me clean up before she got her books out.

After we properly rested, we went into the study and I brought out my books too. We brainstormed the project topics and I was very glad to have had Cindy as a project partner because she was a very brilliant student. We finally agreed on a topic and started the first chapter. It was probably one of my best evenings as I laughed at all of Cindy's jokes. I was also able to stop myself from staring at her like a lovesick puppy. The day also ended with a bang as Cindy asked me to go out with her during the weekend.

Before the weekend finally came, all my friends gave me tips on how to kiss a girl. I had finally dressed up and I assured my parents of my early return. I had expected my parents to refuse but they were happy that I was going out with a girl. Cindy arrived in a taxi and I joined her, still unsure of where we were going as she had decided not to let me know.

"Where are we going?" I asked after fifteen minutes into the car ride. All my friends had put so much fear in my heart by describing a lot of scary places in the city while making me believe Cindy would actually take me one of those places. As if sensing my fear, she decided to put me out of my misery.

"We are going to a roller skate center, my uncle owns the place," Cindy said proudly.

I looked at her long and hard trying to see if she was joking or not. I had never been on a roller skate before and I was sure I was going to embarrass myself.

"Are you being serious?" I asked as I tried to weigh the gravity of the situation and see if it was the right time to run home and forget about her.

"I am serious," Cindy said as she looked at me with her angelic eyes. Those eyes had already begun confusing me and I knew I couldn't really run away at that point.

When we got to the place, I noticed that Cindy did not pay the taxi driver, nor did she allow me to do so. I guessed she must have been pretty familiar with the taxi driver; besides, her bubbly personality looked like one that would have won a lot of hearts over. The entrance to the skating rink was amazing as various colors of light brought the entire place to life. There were several people in the ring and I could hear the loud music blasting from the speakers. Cindy went to meet her uncle and got us our skates; she came back with our skates and I was asked to put them on. I discovered that I was shaking like Scooby Doo did when he saw a ghost, and I felt like I was going to bolt away at any moment. I tried to give myself a pep talk and motivated myself when I saw a bunch of professionals skating in different directions with so much grace and poise. I knew that if I just got into their midst I was prone to injure one of them.

"I don't think I can do this," I finally admitted to Cindy. She talked to me and tried to calm me down and I did not notice when she dragged me into the open rink. The place was huge and my fear of injuring someone gradually faded away as I took the size of the rink into consideration.

The music blared loudly through the speakers and people skated along to the tunes. It was magical.

"What did you say?" I shouted as I could not hear Cindy over the music.

"Just hold on to me and you will be fine." Cindy grinned at me and I decided to let her take control. I wobbled when she moved me forward; her arms were no longer around my side to guide me and I ended up failing to kick up right. I tried to grab onto a pole so I would not end up making us fall, but as she tried to grab a hold of me tighter, I ended up smacking her in the mouth and taking her to the floor with me. We landed with a loud grunt, Cindy lying beside me. We had not even made it to the group of skaters who were skating around in a circle clockwise. My face flamed red when I noticed a bunch of guys and girls staring our way. Some were laughing out right, and some were still trying to hide their amusement.

They were in for more laughs and I wanted to let them know that it was only just the beginning.

"Why don't I just walk while you skate?" I asked hopefully.

"Not allowed unless you're a member of staf," Cindy replied and then grinned. I tried to stand up on my own, but I ended up falling flat on my butt again. I was glad my friends were not around to see me embarrass myself that way.

Cindy held out her hand to help me up and I gratefully took it. When I stood up on my feet again, I dusted my shorts forgetting I had been sitting in a ring and not a dusty floor. *Alright, I can do this. Just one time around the circle, and we can go,* I thought, hoping one circle would be enough to make Cindy happy.

CHAPTER EIGHTEEN

"**D**on't move for a second," she shouted near my ear over the music. I listened to what she said; I really did not want to move, but being on skates was like torture for me as I just seemed to move even without wanting to.

Cindy's uncle came around and promised to teach me how to skate. Soon, he stood behind me and pressed his body slightly against my back, his hands firmly on my side. He kicked my feet together gently, not enough to make me topple, then leaned in again.

"Keep your feet still, don't lift them or try to move. I am going to skate and you're going to ... roll with it," he said, chuckling, the sound deep and husky in my ear. He sounded like Coach Jeff to me.

He started to move and I squealed, and as if with a mind of their own my feet started to separate, sliding away from each other.

"I can't do this," I whined and cursed myself for becoming a girl. You know; the types that whine at the most stupid things.

"Come on, you can do it. Let's try it this way," Cindy said to me before skating effortlessly in front of me. She skidded to a halt, took my hands and started skating backwards.

"Keep your feet together," she shouted and I concentrated hard on keeping my feet together with my hands gripped firmly on her.

We finally made it to the circle and I squealed with happiness. That's when another incident happened. I ended up flying forward, but to catch my balance I used Cindy's hands to pull myself up; at the same time she did the same thing, causing me to fly backwards. I rolled backwards, my arms flailing everywhere and then I landed into a hard body. Before I knew it, I had caused a pile-up in the circle.

Cindy and her uncle skated over to me grinning ear to ear before helping me up from the floor. I looked behind me to apologize but gasped when I saw the person I had bumped into hold his dangly arm grunting in pain. I looked at Cindy, horrified, but she just shook her head and turned away looking amused.

Then I looked properly at the chaos around the person I had hit and felt like crying. A girl not far behind had a nosebleed; another one was clutching her red fingers in pain while yet another person was rubbing frantically at his leg while his head had an egg-shaped lump on it.

"We need to go," I shouted to Cindy before trying to skate off but ended up falling on my knees. Staff members came rushing over to the injured and my face flamed in embarrassment. When one person asked what had happened, the one with what I think was a broken arm turned to me with a thunderous expression. I ripped my skates off, not bothering to pick them up before running out of the hall. I was so embarrassed. Cindy rushed out behind me on her skates, her face full of amusement. She was carrying my skates and I was glad she had, especially when I remembered that I couldn't get my shoes back without them. Cindy returned our skates and she came back with two popsicles.

"How did you know which flavor I liked best?" I asked, surprised at her.

"I saw you lick one in school," she said, blushing.

"Is that so?" I saw this as my opportunity to tease her. "So when did you learn how to skate like that?" I asked.

"Ever since my mother died, she died last year and I was forced to move down here and live with my uncle. Skating was a coping mechanism at first, but I later came to love it," Cindy said freely. I admired her peaceful countenance when she talked.

"I like how free-spirited you are," I said without really thinking.

"Thank you," she said, surprised by the compliment. "I am sorry about today; I should not have pushed you to skate, especially when you had clearly said you were horrible at it," Cindy said sincerely.

"It was fun a bit, especially before I injured almost everyone," I replied, finally finding humor in what I did. "Do you swim?" I asked her.

"No, I don't. I know you swim as I have seen your pictures on the school's hall of fame. I was always curious as to who you were and had assumed you were a senior who had gone to college. This was the main reason why I took your chair since nobody told me you were still in the school," Cindy said as she tried to make me understand her reason for taking the chair.

I was already aware that she had felt bad that day, but I was also very surprised that no one told her the real reason why I was absent. I did not know if she was pretending not to know or if she genuinely did not know. I debated mentally with myself for a few seconds because I didn't know if telling her was a good idea or not. I still wanted us to be friends and I was scared my talking was going to ruin that.

"I know," Cindy said. "Her death was your fault." She took my hands in hers. Hearing her say that alone made me feel better than I had felt for the past year.

CHAPTER NINETEEN

I was a young boy in love and it was the best feeling ever, it was as if everyone could now notice the new glow in my eyes. I also started dreaming again, but this time it was not the horrifying dream I frequently had in the past that often left me dripping in my own sweat. This dream was a better dream as I was with Cindy. We were always seated in a restaurant in my dream and the restaurant was always empty. We would order for our favorite ice cream and combine the two flavors together just to be adventurous.

I would watch Cindy's long black hair dance around as the wind snuck into the restaurant. I would watch her face graduate into a wonderful smile that always seemed to light up my world. She would always wear her favorite socks, which she said were given to her by her dad. The smile often brought out her eyes and I would always tell her that just so I could watch her blush. When we were done with our ice creams, we would go out into the pouring rain and dance like silly monkeys to a Bruno Mars song. I was always happy in this dream and I often never wanted to wake up.

"Hey Ken, wake up," my father said as he removed the duvet from my face. "I have told you to stop covering your face like that when you sleep, it scares me, Son," my father added with a worried look on his face.

"I am sorry, Father," I replied apologetically. Covering my entire body with my duvet while I slept had become a new hobby of mine ever since I lost my sister; however, it always frightened my parents. The first time I tried such a thing my mother screamed so loudly that I woke up as if I was struck by lightning and almost flew out of the bed as I tried not to wet myself.

"You will be in charge of the shop today; I plan on taking your mother out for a romantic dinner and probably a picnic too. It is our anniversary today," my father said excitedly like a schoolboy in love.

"I didn't get you guys anything. I can't believe I forgot something like this," I wailed.

"Well, I am glad you forgot," my father said as he smiled at me.

"What! You are? Why?" I asked, curious.

"You see I need your help to prepare the meals your mother and I will take for the picnic. You know how useless I am with cooking," my father said sheepishly.

My father had almost burnt down the house on a certain Mother's Day in the past. I was very young at that time and my father had promised my mother breakfast in bed. He decided to prepare the famous English breakfast for her but instead made a burnt offering. He had poured too much cooking oil in the pan and had whisked the eggs with a huge chunk of the shell still in them. He had also been unable to measure the salt and mistakenly poured more than a tablespoonful into the mixture. He had also believed that he could simultaneously combine toasting the bread and frying the eggs together; he burnt a whole bag of bread before he finally even settled on just adding butter beside the bread. He also tried tasting the eggs and from the look on his face that day, I knew they were definitely going to be thrashed. He decided to make bacon and sausages when he saw that the eggs were not manageable but ended up setting the oven mitts on fire this time around. My father was so scared of the oil splashing on his body that he maintained a very long distance between himself and the frying pan.

This only resulted in the sausages and bacon burning before he could get to turn them. When my father had realized what was happening, he tried to reduce the flame coming from the gas burner; however, this had the opposite effect as he increased the flames instead. The fire then spread to the ovens instead and my father danced anxiously like a ballerina. My mother had been unaware of the situation until the sprinklers went off because of the fire. My mother and father spent the whole day cleaning up and we eventually went out for lunch instead.

"So what meal do you have in mind? My excellent cooking skills are at your service," I announced proudly to my father.

"Please climb down from that high horse, you got that excellent cooking skill from me, young man. It just happens that I can no longer cook. But when I was your age, I used to win so many cooking shows," My father said, exaggerating.

I burst into a huge fit of laughter when I saw my father's face as he announced such an accomplishment.

"Okay ... okay," I said, trying to hold in the laughter. "Where exactly is Mother?" I asked.

"I sent her to the spa, she should be there for more than an hour so that gives us enough time to cook, right?"

"Well, you still have not told me what we will be cooking

yet though," I said to my father as I straightened up my bed and headed into the bathroom to brush my teeth.

"I was thinking of something fancy, something that will definitely knock her socks off," my father said dreamily.

"Why do I feel like this journey into the land of our kitchen will not end well?" I said teasingly.

"Hey young man, do not jinx things yet," my father said as he walked towards me and dragged me out of the room.

My father and I walked gingerly to the kitchen; it was already in a mess, which showed that my father had already tried experimenting with a recipe.

"Okay, so be honest. What exactly were you trying to make that turned the kitchen upside down like this?" I asked him inquisitively.

"I only tried to heat up the soy sauce, just like I have seen your mother do." My father said this like it was the greatest achievement of his life.

I was shocked at the number of pans that seemed to be out and I wondered how my father had managed to use all of them. This occurrence still remains a mystery to me to this day because my father was unable to give an explanation for it.

"So first of all we will start by washing off these pans. Wait, where exactly is the soy sauce you heated?" I asked my father when I found no evidence of any heated sauce.

"It is nonexistent," my father replied shyly.

"I do not get it... How is that even possible?" I asked, alarmed once again.

"You know how cooking and I do not seem to agree with each other..."

"Yes," I said in a loud voice, cutting my father off in the middle of his statement.

He rolled his eyes before he continued.

"So I tried to let it simmer like I have seen your mother do, but I had forgotten that I was expected to lower the heat. What is so funny?" my father asked when he caught me snickering behind my palm.

"I really can't believe you burnt the soy sauce," I said, unable to contain my laughter.

"Whatever, let's get down to business," my father said as he opened the dishwasher.

Once we were all done with washing the pans, my father and I decided on a little meal to make. I gave him some fresh oranges and other fruits to squeeze, the plan was to make a fruit punch. I knew there was no way my father was going to mess up the fruit punch. I decided to bring out some of the already made pastries that my mother had stored in the fridge and heated them up in our oven. I also made some pasta and meatball sauce since my mother was a pasta fan. Soon enough we were done cooking and my father and I packed the picnic basket properly. It was a wonderful sight to behold and I was glad we had in so much effort into doing something special. I asked my father to go up and get ready since I knew he was going to take forever doing so.

I was cleaning up the kitchen when I heard my mother come in; she looked so relaxed and was happy she had been able to treat herself like royalty. She was a very hard worker and I was happy that she at least got days like this to sit back and enjoy herself.

"Welcome Mother," I said as I walked up to meet her. I had forgotten the apron I was wearing as I hugged her and I tried not to stain her beautiful dress with the stains on the apron.

"What exactly are you up to, my young chef?" my mother said as she bent down to kiss my forehead.

"Nothing much, just creating something special for your special day," I said mischievously. "Happy anniversary, Mother, you look absolutely stunning." I watched her twirl and laugh.

"Thank you, Ken. Where is your father?" she asked inquisitively.

"He is upstairs, taking a shower."

"Are you sure that is all he is doing?" my mother asked as she looked at me pointedly.

"Yes, I believe so."

"Your father has been acting so shady today; it is hard to know what he is up to," she said, smiling like a schoolgirl.

"Really? I hadn't noticed," I said innocently.

My mother just looked at me with her side eye before going upstairs to meet my dad.

I used the little free time I had to text Cindy. Communication between us had become stronger and I was not sure if I was meant to ask her to be my girlfriend yet. We had gone out just twice and I didn't want to rush things with her, she had made my life more colorful and I was not sure I was ready to lose her as a friend yet. Kevin was pressuring me to ask her out and he was always trying to make me bump into her whenever I saw her in the hallway. I opened my phone and saw that I already had a text message from Cindy; she had texted to let me know that she had started reading a book I had given her. She sent more texts as she continued to read the book and I laughed as I read her responses. I gave her a book by Sidney Sheldon and she was already threatening to jump to the end of the book to find out who the killer was. I had to convince her to hold on and enjoy the book before she thought about skipping it, she later promised she was going to try her best to do so then told me she had dropped some love stickers on her favorite pages of the book. I tried to make sense of what that meant before my parents walked into my room to hurry me up so they could drop me off at the shop.

"You look so lovely, Mother," I said to my mother who was dressed in a long flowing yellow gown. She was also wearing tiny earrings, which seemed to shimmer under the light, I had not seen her wear them before and I could only assume that my father had just given them to her as one of his many gifts.

"What about me?" my father said in his whining voice as he twirled around like a girl also.

"You also look lovely, Father, your shoes match your outfit perfectly," I said as I looked at the cool shoes my father was wearing.

"Thanks Ken. We leave in five minutes so get ready so we can drop you off at the bakery first. I have written down things I would like you to help us do on the iPad and will put you through once you are done getting ready.

CHAPTER TWENTY

My mother's bakery was one of the busiest places in our whole town on Saturdays and this was why my mother was not too happy about leaving me alone to supervise it. The bakery had become so popular in our town that people often trooped in on Saturdays to have their breakfast; my mother's breakfast menu was one of a kind as you could have extras without having to pay extra. Customers who came in on Saturdays were often too stuffed and most times found it difficult to leave their seats. There was also a magazine and newspaper stand in the shop where customers often settled in to discuss politics or the latest gossip.

Today was no different as I could already see people trooping into the bakery when I alighted from my parents' car. My mother had repeatedly told me to call her if anything happened and, although I promised to do just that, she still wanted to get down from the car when we stopped at the bakery. It was a funny sight to witness as my father threatened to carry her back into the car before she finally agreed to leave.

The smell of my mother's shop was one I could never forget even to this day, it was one of those smells that was forever imprinted in my nose. My mother's bakery was one of those bakeries that could make you hungry even if you had no plans of eating. The tantalizing aroma of the hot pastries and coffee was enough to make you salivate. Kevin often fell victim to the smell of the bakery, and no matter how stuffed he was before entering he was still always tempted to still request an éclair.

I walked through the back of the bakery as I was already late, I already knew there was no way I was going to pass through the front without being pulled by a customer who would want to find out how I was doing. The back of the bakery was the second entrance into the kitchen and it was only used by employees, each employee had their own key, which they submitted when the shop closed and picked up when they arrived each day.

The kitchen was one of the busiest parts of the bakery. The six bakers that worked for my mother were always busy and the only time they got a break was when their shift was over. The kitchen was very spacious and it could contain a party of fifty guests comfortably, this was because my mother had always hated small spaces as she was claustrophobic.

"Please pass me that five-kilogram measure butter in that pan, please," Jean said. Jean had been one of my mother's most loyal bakers, he was a well-sought-after baker in both the United States and France but had decided to stick with my mother's bakery. The day I heard of his popularity, I came to understand fully why my mother's shop was a favorite tourist eatery. Jean had been poached by a lot of top bakeries and this had often made my mother worry a lot; however, he had proven himself on countless occasions by sticking with my mother's little bakery.

"Here it is," I said as I handed over the butter to Jean so he could add it into his mixture.

"I heard you are my boss today, oui?" Jean said as we both washed our hands together.

"Not really," I said shyly.

"Nonsense, I will make sure everyone listens to you," Jean said. He proceeded to ring a little bell, which I had not known existed, and everyone stopped what they were doing to listen to him. He was the head baker and had total command of the activities in the kitchen.

"I have an announcement to make, guys. Ken here is in charge of the bakery today, so all issues should be reported to him," Jean said in his very thick French accent. "Any questions?"

In unison they all said no.

"Let us get back to work then, travailler dur," Jean told them as he handed me an apron.

I collected the apron and walked into an office where I met Travis. Travis was the overall general manager of the bakery and was happy to show me the ropes once Jean handed me over to him. The bakery was still very packed even at that hour and I was shocked at the amount of behind-the-scenes activities that went down in running the bakery. All these days I came to the bakery, I had assumed it was a piece of cake since all I ever did was serve the customers and most times I even got huge tips when they discovered I was Sarah's son. Today, things were different as I noticed the activities that went on behind the counter. There was a sudden rush in everyone's step; then I noticed the coffee machine was broken, so the coffee was taking a longer period to get ready. I also noticed that some customers got angry when they did not get their orders on time and Travis had to go to them to smooth things over with them. At some point some of them had to just settle for tea and the juice option on the menu. Everything felt overwhelming but I was glad I could assist in my own little way. My parents arrived from their date late in the night, we were already closing up and most of the staff had already gone home.

"Welcome madame. You look very lovely tonight," Jean called out to my mother as soon as she walked into the bakery.

"Thank you, Jean," my mother replied, smiling. She looked very happy and I could tell that she had a great time.

"Why does everyone keep forgetting me?" my father grumbled again.

"You are the most handsome man on Earth," Travis and Jean both chorused as they tried to stifle their laughter.

"Now you guys just took it too far," my father said, joining in the laughter.

"So how did today go?" my mother called out to Jean and Travis as she began to walk into her office.

Travis and Jean both followed my mother into the office, while my father and I tried to clean up the places that still needed to be tidied up.

"Almost forgot, Kevin will be coming over tonight. Mr. Greg is currently in the hospital and he said he does not want to stay with his cousin. He also mentioned that he had been trying to reach you since."

I had activated my phone's airplane mode ever since I started working, and so I turned it off and saw about twelve missed calls from Kevin. I immediately returned his call as I excused myself.

"Kevin, what's up?"

"Were you and Cindy doing some fishy business? I called you so many times," Kevin said teasingly.

"Oh please... How is Mr. Greg? What exactly is happening?"

"You mean that old man, he is in the hospital. That man wants to give me a heart attack at my young age," Kevin said in a dramatic way.

"What happened?" I asked, panicking.

"He was break dancing and tripped on a stool."

"What?" I said, surprised, as I also tried to hold my laughter.

"Yup, he was trying to copy some dancers on YouTube and ended up doing himself harm."

"Did the doctor say he will be alright?" I asked worriedly.

"He will be fine; the doctor just wants to keep him for a few days just to ensure he is okay. I trust my grandfather to be home in a day's time," Kevin said.

"Glad he is fine. So where are you now?"

"In front of your house," Kevin said.

"But there is no one home," I told him, just in case he was oblivious to that fact.

"I know that, waiting for you to bring your ass home. I already spoke to your parents."

"Oh ...we are currently waiting for my mother to finish up. We would be home soon."

"Could you help me bring five éclairs, my dearest friend?" Kevin said, trying to sound nice.

"What exactly do you need five for?" I asked, laughing at Kevin's request.

"I am very hungry. The last time I ate was like two o'clock, the Kevin engine runs on food as fuel so ... would you bring them?"

"Today is Saturday so there are really no leftovers in the shop, so I am so sorry to disappoint the Kevin engine."

"Noooooooooooo, so is this how the story of my first heartbreak will be written," Kevin wailed on the phone loudly.

I had to take the phone away from my ears to avoid my ear drums falling off.

"Fear not, the Kevin engine shall be filled up," I said.

"Hurry," Kevin said, sounding very excited.

When I returned to where my father had been cleaning, I discovered he was done and soon enough we all ended up in the car and were heading home.

CHAPTER TWENTY-ONE

Kevin was seated on our front porch by the time we pulled up into our driveway, he was already dressed in his batman pajamas, which he had grown out of but still insisted on wearing.

"Happy anniversary!" Kevin said as soon as he saw my parents.

"Thank you, Kevin. Sorry about the delay," my mother said.

"It is fine, ma'am," Kevin said sweetly. He always pretended to be a saint whenever he came to my house and if Mr. Greg was not a friend of my parents they would have believed his gentle saint act.

"What would you guys like for dinner, so I can get a start on it?" my mother asked Kevin and me.

"Anything would be fine with me, Mother," I said, not particularly interested in food. This was no longer unusual because ever since my sister died, food had no longer held the same type of appeal to me as it used to. I used to be a big foodie as a child; I could eat an adult's portion even before I was a year old. My father had previously assumed I would grow up to become an obese child but was surprised when I grew up to be skinny. My mother once told me a story of how I ate like a whale as a child and I threw into my mouth anything that crossed my path. She told me of the wonderful day I had eaten all the buttons on the remote control leaving them to initially assume that it was a rat until I fell sick. The chemicals of the buttons had greatly upset my stomach and I was rushed to the hospital. Although the story sounded funny now, I could always see my mother heave a sigh of relief whenever she told it to anyone.

My sister had been like me and had loved eating as long as there were no vegetables on her plate. She even hated the color green so much because they were the colors of her worst food. I, on the other hand, loved everything food and I also enjoyed making it. I often took Star along with me to the kitchen and would place her on a stool as she watched me cook. She was always a great cooking companion as she asked a lot of funny questions. There was a time when she begged me to let her assist me in cooking, and despite the numerous kitchen accidents that almost happened on that day, I still consider it to be one of my happiest memories in the kitchen. We had made curry sauce and some rice and Star had wanted to assist me in the process. She had helped wash the rice to remove any excess starch that might have still been in it and she had poured some liquid in it when I was not looking. If she had not told me she wanted to play with the bubbles in the rice, we would have had very high chances of tasting dish washing liquid for the first time that day.

She had also passed me sugar when I asked her for salt and had begged to be allowed to pour it in the pot. I still believe that if I had not insisted that we both pour the salt together she would have ended up pouring all the sugar into the sauce and we all would have gotten sick the next day.

On that day, I left left the kitchen while Star was seated in her high chair beside the kitchen counter. I did not know that she had gotten hold of the olive oil and had poured half of its contents on the floor. When I came running in to check on the burning rice, I slipped on the ground. I was lucky enough to have landed on the kitchen rug instead of on the hard, cold tile. I saw my life flash before my eyes that day as my head resounded on the tile floor. I just looked dazed on the ground as I stared blankly into space. It was not until Star started to cry that I found the strength to stand up and attend to her screams. The rice was salvaged as I was able to put off the gas cooker before the entire food burnt. The kitchen accident, however, had not stopped there as Star touched the hot cover of the pot with the sole aim of playing with it but ended up sustaining a burn on her hand. That day was a very eventful day for Star and me as we had both laughed and cried together. We had eaten from the same plate as we watched Sponge Bob. Things had, however, changed since her death and I no longer looked forward to cooking or eating.

"I would like your delicious pasta, ma'am," Kevin said, bringing me back to the present.

"No problem then, you boys go on upstairs. I will call you when dinner is ready."

"Thanks, ma'am."

"Thanks, Mother," I said, shaking my head as I looked at Kevin who suddenly became hyper because of food. If there was one thing he loved more than basketball, it was food. Kevin was never satisfied with whatever food was served in the cafeteria and always packed an extra bag of lunch just to get satisfied. On days when he didn't pack an extra lunch, we, his friends, often suffered for it as Kevin would ask for our food to be shared.

"Tell me you brought comics?" I asked Kevin as soon as he made himself comfortable on my bed.

"When have I not brought comics?" Kevin said, offended.

"The time we were at Becky's place; the first time I invited Lance for our sleepover..."

"You store all those moments up in your head, I am not impressed," Kevin said with a pout.

"Let us start with that or should we watch a movie first?" I asked Kevin.

"I thought you were heading into the bathroom?" Kevin asked, surprised.

"I am actually," I replied.

"Why exactly are we discussing this now?"

"I like planning," I replied, shocked that Kevin had not noticed that before.

"Since when did you become the master planner? The time you spent planning could have been used in having a quick shower. Although you stink, I don't think a quick shower is ideal in the picture," Kevin said as he held his nose.

I had zoned out on Kevin as I made my way to the bathroom thinking of what he said. To me, planning came naturally as it helped me put things in order. If I planned this, I knew the chances of things going wrong would not be as high as if I did not plan at all. However, I started to realize that I only developed this habit when my sister died. I had needed a form of order in my life and planning things according to a schedule both physical and mentally had greatly helped me feel more in control and also deal with my panic attacks. I already had a routine and this helped me greatly as I preferred to know things beforehand so I could plan them properly and fit them into my schedule.

"Your mum says the food is ready!" Kevin screamed out to me from the bathroom door. I knew that a few minutes from now he would start trying to hurry me up, and my predictions were right as Kevin had already helped me to pick out my favorite pajamas.

"Are you that hungry?" I asked Kevin when I saw the clothes already arranged on the bed.

"Yes, is that not what I have been trying to tell you?" Kevin wailed. He was already looking impatient and I could see the temptation to leave me and go and start dinner alone in his eyes. I knew he would not do that, though, because Kevin was a very respectful boy and he often tried to pretend to be a saint when he had a sleepover. The real Kevin, however, came out when he was at home with Mr. Greg instead. I knew that if the case was reversed and we were in Kevin's home, the probability of him resisting any form of temptation relating to food was very low.

"I am dressing as fast as I can," I said to Kevin, who was eyeing me as he glanced through an *Academy Fighter* comic book.

"Was spraying that perfume necessary? Or do you have a secret date with Cindy that you are not telling me about?"

I just rolled my eyes at Kevin in response as we both headed downstairs. Dinner was already served and I had noted that there were just two plates on the dining table. As if sensing my curiosity, my mother walked towards the dining table.

"Your father and I are stuffed and will be going to bed now, so you guys should clean up and go to your rooms after," my mother said as she hugged Kevin and me.

"Let's go," she called out to my father who was engrossed in the television.

"But ... they were just getting to the best part," my father said as he was forced to switch off the television and go to bed.

"You can record it and watch it later," my mother suggested.

"It would not be the same," my father said as he tried to hide his yawn.

"I know you would end up dozing off while the television plays, so please let's just go to bed now. I can tell that you are very tired," my mother said affectionately.

"Goodnight boys," my father said.

"Goodnight sir."

"Goodnight Father."

When Kevin was sure my parents had gone to bed, he began to squeal like a girl in excitement.

"Oh my God, your mother is literally the best cook on this planet. We should send our chef over here to learn from her," he said with a mouth full of spaghetti.

"You need to tell me where she gets this sauce from because I have not tasted anything like it. It is beyond mind-blowing," he said as he continued wolfing down the spaghetti.

My mother was an amazing cook and this was one of the reasons why I always loved the kitchen in the past. When I was ten years of age, I had dreams of becoming a chef and that was one thing I proudly told people whenever they asked me who I wanted to be like. Things had changed as I now wanted to become a doctor. I wanted the ability to save lives and help those who needed medical help. I was not sure of what the next ten years were going to hold for me at that point, but I knew that whatever profession I chose, I wanted to be able to help people, especially children who did not have, just like my parents were doing at that time. My parents belonged to so many charity organizations and they were often silent donators. Their contributions to most of these organizations often went a long way towards reaching the founder's goal and it often made them happy to see their dreams being actualized.

"Are you going to finish that?" Kevin asked as he pointed to my huge chicken laps.

"I have not even touched it, and when did you finish yours so fast? Where are the bones?" I asked as all those questions kept flying through my head.

"Calm down," Kevin said as he smiled. I saw the bones sticking out from the side of his mouth. "They are still here, do you want some?" Kevin said as he brought out the chicken lap bone from his mouth.

"Eeeeeew," I said as I watched him ruin my meal. "Did you feel the need to bring it out of your mouth?" I asked, alarmed.

"You wanted me to swallow that huge bone?" Kevin asked, pretending to be shocked even though he had on countless occasions attempted to do just that.

"You are free to have half of my chicken after I have taken my portion. I do not trust you with my chicken lap to allow you to take a bite first," I said as I eyed Kevin like a predator about to pounce on its prey. I recalled my last experience with him and how I had tried sharing an ice cream cone with him. That was one of my worst ideas; I blamed myself when my ice cream was gone.

I had gone through the stress of queuing for that particular flavor as it was a mixture of so many flavors and always knocked my socks off whenever I had it. However, on that day, I had promised to share with Kevin as he arrived late and was still at the far end of the queue. I had gotten the ice cream and even gotten a spoon to make the sharing easier, but Kevin, who had other plans, had swallowed the whole ice cream on the cone. He pleaded that it was a mistake, but it was a mistake that I had never forgotten.

When we were done eating, we went into the kitchen to wash the dishes before neatly stacking them in their appropriate places. I was able to tell that Kevin was over-stuffed from the sluggish way he worked. I knew he was going to sleep it off in no time.

"So which one have you decided? Are we reading the new comic books you brought? Wait, they are new comics, right?" I turned to ask Kevin as we neared the door to my room.

"I am not sure," Kevin said with a shrug.

"What do you mean you are not sure?" I asked, sounding like a spoilt child. Comic books had been one of my very close companions after the death of my sister, and I had spent days in my room imagining myself to be my favorite superhero. She was a woman, but that did not still stop me from making her my favorite.

She had healing powers and she was always sought after whenever there was a huge battle going on. Her powers were as great as the fastest and the strongest superhero because without her they would all die. My parents had also made it their duty during that time to always get me a new edition of the comic that came out. They noticed that it was the only thing that could make me come out of my room and probably utter a few sentences.

"Just check them out," Kevin said as he slumped on my bed and hugged one of my pillows tightly.

I opened the comics one by one as I flipped through them. It was hard to just flip through them, especially since they were new ones I had not seen before. When I noticed that Kevin had dozed off, I got comfortable as I read each page and got pulled into the world where superheroes were real. As I continued to read, I felt a huge thud on my head that immediately caused me to drop the comic book I was reading.

"What was that for?" I asked as I turned my head and noticed that it was Kevin who threw a pillow at my head.

"What do you think you are doing?" he asked.

"Reading a comic, what does it look like?" I replied.

"I thought we were meant to read that together. I had even meant to choose between reading the comic books and watching television," Kevin asked.

"Well, that was meant to be your choice until you decided to doze off right on the bed. I was not sure if you were still going to wake up today, especially with the way you ate this evening."

"What do you mean?" Kevin asked, trying to act offended as he threw yet another pillow at me.

"Is it your plan to give me a migraine?" I asked Kevin who looked like he was in the process of throwing another pillow at my face.

"Well, you deserve it. How many have you read so far?" Kevin asked as he rubbed the last bit of sleep from his eyes.

"Not so much," I said, lying.

"Please expatiate on your not so much. Thank you."

"Just four," I replied.

"Just four, I only brought five and I can guess you are reading the fifth one," Kevin said accusingly.

"Kind of. Hey, don't you dare throw that pillow," I said to Kevin who had grabbed another pillow immediately I replied.

"So we have to get into a compromise now that you have ruined what we were meant to read together," Kevin said with a glint in his eyes. I already knew he was up to something with just that look.

"So what exactly is going on here?" I asked, suddenly curious as to what Kevin had up his sleeves.

"Sit up properly so you can face me," Kevin instructed with his serious face on.

I suddenly became scared as he hardly ever used that face around me except when he had some sad news or he was analyzing basketball.

"Is something wrong?" I asked, worried that something disastrous might have happened.

"Nothing is wrong. I just wanted to talk to you about something."

"What is happening, Kev?"

"It is about Cindy—"

"What about her?" I asked, interrupting Kevin as I felt my heart beat faster and faster.

"Nothing is wrong with her, so please do not look like that," Kevin said.

"Just talk."

"We all think you should ask her out," Kevin said without blinking.

"What?" I asked.

"We all think you should ask her out," Kevin said again, this time in a louder voice.

"I heard you the first time. You did not have to repeat yourself."

"I didn't know that."

"Wait, you said we. Who is the WE?" I asked Kevin.

"Tee, Becky, Paul, and even Lance," Kevin said.

"Wow, I find it hard to believe that Lance agreed to this," I said, shocked.

"Well, he did. You know ever since he started dating Summer, I believe the very soft side of him has started to show."

"LANCE HAS A GIRLFRIEND! AND IT IS SUMMER?" I asked, shocked that such information had passed me by.

"Yeah, he does, although he just started dating her recently."

"Why did I not know of this?"

Kevin remained silent for a minute.

"You have not been accessible and no one has really gotten to talk to you for a year. We are all just happy we are getting to speak to you now and none of us want to ruin that by discussing our personal life problems," Kevin said sadly.

I looked at Kevin for a few minutes as I tried to register what he had said. I had not really realized that my friends were treating me like an egg and I could not blame them. I had pushed them away from me for a whole year and I was grateful they had still wanted to be my friends afterward. I can remember days when they had turned up at my doorstep and I had still refused to see them or days when they would request a video call and I would deny their request. I was in a dark place and they had all still tried to be there for me. Lance still often gave me news about the various swimming teams and I was always still updated despite my never replying to him. Kevin was always talking to me like I was replying to him and this had made me smile on several occasions. I knew I owed my friends a lot as they had saved me on one occasion when I had become extremely suicidal.

On that day, I had been extremely tired of life. My father and mother had started fighting and arguing over every little thing and they had become bitter towards each other. It was like none of us cared about life again and we were just ghosts floating around aimlessly. That day, I snuck some of my parents' pills from their room when they were in one of their heated arguments again and they had not even noticed me walk in and leave. I poured like ten pills from different bottles into my hand and I was about to swallow them when I received a notification on my laptop. It was a message from my friends. I had hesitated to open the message because I had felt I was going to change my mind about killing myself. However, I still held the pills in my hands so I decided to leave them a farewell message instead. I clicked on their message to ignore what they had sent as I typed my farewell speech. Instead, the video they sent as a message played instantly.

They had all sat in Tee's living room in an arrangement that looked like they wanted to snap a family portrait. That alone made me laugh and I was sure they knew this because I told them on countless occasions how I hated professional pictures because of the seating arrangement. In the video, they all talked one after another and they all let me know how much they loved me and missed me.

They had ended the video with a song as they tried to act like a boy band. They sounded terrible and I had laughed until I had ended up crying. They had argued after as they all blamed each other for the terrible sound that was coming out of the speaker. I had stopped midway through their argument and ran to my parents' room feeling overwhelmed. I even told them what I had tried to do and they broke down as they could not believe that they had been too engrossed in their problems and had not been able to notice how depressed I had become. That day was a day I can never forget even to date and I had agreed that my friends were amazing people who I could never take for granted.

"I am in a much better place now, thanks to all of you, so you guys can come to me with anything," I said to Kevin.

"So will you ask Cindy out?" Kevin asked eagerly.

"I still can't believe you guys sat down and had a discussion about this," I said, laughing at the ridiculousness of how the whole thing must have played out.

"I am tempted to throw a pillow at you, so please stop laughing," Kevin said as he also began to chuckle.

"Okay, I will stop," I said as I tried to hold in my laughter. "I do not know how I feel about asking her out," I finally admitted to Kevin.

"We all think she makes you happy and we always see a different side of you when you are around her."

"Really?"

"Yes, if we had not noticed that, we would not have thought of telling you this."

"I do not know if my heart is ready for that, what if she says no?" I asked Kevin.

"At least you asked, and rejections are a part of life."

"Did Kevin just sound philosophical or are my ears deceiving me?" I cried out to the room.

"You are just making things weird here," Kevin said, laughing.

"I do not think my heart can love another person, not after what happened to Star. I don't think I want to try anything that would hurt me at the end of the day."

"Well, you will not know if you do not try it," Kevin said.

"You are on a roll today, Kevin," I said as I clapped my hands loudly.

"So will you think about it?" Kevin asked.

"Yea, I will," I replied.

"So when will you be done thinking about it?"

"Are you seriously asking me to give you a time, Kevin?"

"Well, not really. There's no rush. But you know Valentine's Day is coming soon, we do not want another guy to steal her from your hands," Kevin said, baiting me as he caught my curiosity.

"Do you think there is a guy who wants to ask her out?" I asked Kevin, curious as to what his reply might be.

"More than one guy actually, I have heard some guys on my team talk about her a lot and how they wish they had gotten to speak to her first before you came around. These are just guys on my team alone, so you can guess how many more guys from other departments in school might also want her to be theirs.

I think the only thing that is stopping them from going to approach her is because they think you guys are an item already and also because you are the school's golden boy, so I do not think anyone wants to look for trouble with you."

I saw the looks boys gave Cindy whenever she walked through the hallway and, although I had not read so much meaning into it, I was glad Kevin had brought it to my notice.

"I think I will ask her out tomorrow," I said.

"Tomorrow? Is that not too early?" Kevin said, trying to look surprised even though he was the one who had dropped the idea in my head.

"Yes tomorrow, Kevin, and wipe that surprised look off your face," I said.

"Give me a moment. Let me text the boys."

"It's past ten," I said to Kevin.

"Yes, I know," Kevin said as he grabbed his phone and continued to text.

"Wait, did they all stay up this late to hear my response?" I asked, knowing it was something they might do.

"Aww, you know us too well," Kevin said as he came over to hug me.

"Let me see," I said, taking the phone from his hand.

"You guys created a group chat for this?" I asked, sounding very shocked.

"That was the fastest way to communicate, you should not sound so surprised," Kevin said as if that was justifiable.

Soon enough his phone began to buzz.

"Yaaaas, this is good news," Becky had sent with a dancing football player sticker.

"Puppy is excited too, I made him wait up to hear this," Tee texted, sounding weird as usual.

"Glad you were able to convince him. I didn't think you had it in you," Paul had texted.

"Was this group really necessary?" Lance had asked.

I laughed at his reply because it was exactly my reaction.

"You all should go and sleep." I sent it back after signing my name so they would know it was me with the phone.

"We can't wait to hear the good news," Becky texted after.

"You guys heard the boy, go to sleep," Lance texted almost immediately.

"Well, you were not meant to see all that," Kevin said as he went back to his sleeping position. "But it doesn't really matter if you did; we just want you to be happy," he said in between yawns as he drifted back to sleep again.

That night, before I finally drifted off too, I sent a text to Cindy inviting her on a date. I knew if I was going to ask her out, I needed to do it properly. I had never really thought about asking her to be my girlfriend until now. I had always just assumed we were going to be friends for a long time. I had also not thought about her having a boyfriend and as I thought about it that night, I realized that I was very jealous at that thought. However, I was scared about the next day and this was something I hated. I hated fear a lot because it often showed me how weak I was. I was also scared of how things could turn out to be. If Cindy said no, I knew that could be the end of our friendship and I did not want that to happen. I was not ready to lose another person dear to me. I also decided to pick out what to wear for the date as I had found out that planning things helped a lot.

That night, as I dreamt, I saw Star and Cindy playing together. They looked like they had known each other for a long time. I tried to run to meet them, but no matter how much I tried to get to the point they were I was still held back by a shield. I also tried calling their names but neither of them could hear me. It was like they were lost in their little world. I tried tirelessly to call out to them until they both began to fade away little by little. I woke up from this dream with a scream, not loud enough to wake up Kevin, though, as all he did was change position and continue sleeping. I grabbed the paper bag I had stuffed in a cupboard beside my bed and practiced my breathing routine in it. After a few minutes, I discovered that my breathing had returned to normal and so I checked my phone to see what the time was. It was already 6:00 a.m. and I knew I still had a few hours to continue with my sleep, although I had lost interest in sleeping after the scary dream I had. I checked my messages instead and saw a message from Cindy. She wanted to know where we were going and also why I had woken up so late. I had replied immediately telling her the venue and hoped she was still awake. A minute later, I heard my phone notification go up. She had replied and we began to text back and forth.

"That is a fancy place. Now I have to look for what to wear and did my text wake you?"

"I am sure you would look nice in anything and no, I was kind of already awake."

"Are you flirting with me, Ken? <Winking emoji>"

"I was just stating the obvious. < Blushing emoji>"

"You forgot to indicate the time, smarty pants."

"I was too anxious. Sorry about that. Is 11:00 a.m. okay with you?"

"Yes, I will be ready before then. What was making you too anxious?"

"Nothing really, I am fine now. I will be coming to pick you up, well my dad and I will."

"You know you can tell me anything, but if you are sure you are fine then there is no problem. I can't wait to see you."

"I can't wait either. See you soon."

"Got to go now. I need to hunt for a dress for a fancy restaurant."

I smiled to myself as I read the last text from Cindy. I found myself falling back to sleep and this time around, my sleep was more peaceful.

CHAPTER TWENTY-TWO

"**W**ake up Ken." I heard a voice call out to me. I woke up to see my hands around Kevin's body. I must have hugged him as I slept and I immediately flung him off my side of the bed when I noticed this.

"Is this how you treat your lover?" Kevin cried out as he held his heart.

"Oh, please. What just happened never really happened. You shall not speak of it again. Promise me," I pleaded.

"You mean the passionate moment we just shared?" Kevin asked.

"There was no passionate moment, Kevin."

"You hurt my feelings, Ken, and I don't know how you expect me to keep such a moment a secret."

I just sighed and left the bed knowing that arguing with Kevin was not how I would love to start my day. I was also embarrassed about the whole scenario and walked into the bathroom instead.

"Cindy said she is ready," Kevin screamed from the room.

"What?" I asked, unable to hear him as I was under the shower.

"I said Cindy is ready," Kevin said as he walked into the bathroom. "Where are you guys going?"

"Are you really in the bathroom with me right now?" I asked, alarmed.

"Yes, I had to pee and I could not go all the way to the guest bathroom to do that. You can't be shy, not after the passionate moment we just shared," Kevin said teasingly as he walked out of the bathroom.

"I TOLD YOU WE HAD NO PASSIONATE MOMENT," I shouted, hoping I wouldn't see Kevin telling everyone in school such a story.

I later heard him laugh as I continued to shower.

"Please can you pass me my phone?" I asked as I dried the water off my hair.

"Sure," Kevin said as he threw the phone absent-mindedly.

I checked the time and discovered that it was already 10:30 a.m.

"Oh shit. Shit!" I said as I hurriedly pulled out the clothes I had planned to wear that day. I was glad I had gotten them ready as I would have been extra late if I had not done so.

"What is wrong with you?" Kevin said, looking very alarmed as he saw me run around the room like a crazy person as I tried to get ready.

"I told Cindy our date was going to be by eleven and yet I am still not ready even by this time. I have also not told my parents about going out and I don't know who will drive me," I said in a panic-filled voice.

"Take a chill pill, Ken, this thing is not as complicated as you are making it out to be. You are already almost dressed. We can also just call Tee and have his driver come and pick you and Cindy up. While I confirm this, you can dash to your parents' room and seek their permission. I think that is about everything, right?"

"You are a lifesaver, Kevin," I said as I gave him a bro hug.

"Awwww, our passion-filled morning did not just end there," Kevin said as he leaned in for a long hug.

"You just like making things weird," I said as I hurried out of my room and went to see my parents.

"Well, they agreed, what did Tee say?" I asked when I got back.

"His driver is on his way to pick you up. He also said he wanted some of your mother's scones."

"The way you two consume pastries, though, it is a big wonder the two of you are not obese."

"Stop hating and just admit that we both have amazing bodies," Kevin said as he twirled around like a girl.

"So what is your plan once I leave?" I asked Kevin; I had not thought about what he was going to be doing once I left, I had been too engrossed in my problems.

"Paul is coming over and we will head to the hospital to visit my grandpa, I called the hospital and he is already kicking up a storm there. I knew they would not be able to keep him for long," Kevin said laughing.

The relationship between Mr. Greg and Kevin was one I had always admired. Most times it was hard to tell that Mr. Greg was not Kevin's father especially if you didn't consider his age. They both liked the same things and were both equally good at basketball.

The first time I saw Mr. Greg play, my mouth had been left hanging as I had been unable to believe such an old man could play as well as he did. I knew I was a novice when he was in basketball and I would never have dreamt of competing with him.

"I still don't see why you didn't just ask her out over the phone. That is what I did with my girl," Kevin said.

Kevin and his girlfriend had been dating ever since they were eleven, their relationship was quite different from mine as both their parents knew each other and had probably planned their wedding together long before their birth. When Kevin had been transferred down to Green Springs, Christy's parents had done the same and had sent her to Green Springs too. The two of them had previously been at each other's throats when they had been kids, but they had been able to grow on each other.

"Not every girl is Christy, I am still surprised she said yes to your ass," I said teasingly.

"You mean my irresistible self? I do not know how anyone could say no to me," Kevin said as he flexed his muscles.

"Kevin, Paul is here," my mother called out to him.

"Mr. Irresistible will be going to the hospital smelly."

"Never, I have to take a shower. Please help me stall Paul," Kevin pleaded.

"You know Paul does not like to be kept waiting, so I do not know what magic you want me to perform."

"Tell him about our night of passion," Kevin joked.

"I am not moving an inch if you do not promise never to mention that to anyone."

"I can't believe you want to do this right now," Kevin said, sounding pained.

"Oh please, drop the act. Do you promise or not? Time is ticking and Paul will march up here if you do not answer fast."

"Fine, I promise. But this is not the end," Kevin said as he laughed like an evil character in one of our favorite shows.

After a few minutes, he came down to meet Paul who was

in a heated debate with me over which soda was best. As soon as Kevin arrived, Tee's driver also pulled into our driveway and I said my goodbyes to both of them before I entered the car. We were already ten minutes behind schedule and I had sent a text to Cindy apologizing for this. Her house was not so far away and we were there in no time. She was already waiting on her porch and I felt my eyes light up immediately when I saw her. She was dressed in a blue gown with a white flowery pattern on it. She had tied her hair up in a bun and I could still see some stubborn strands try to fight their way out. When she entered, I could smell the sweet aroma of the perfume she was wearing, she smelt like vanilla. She looked so angelic and small at the same time.

"You look so pretty," I told her the moment she got comfortable in the car.

"Thanks, it took a lot of YouTube videos before I could get my hair styled properly," she said as she patted her hair gently.

"It looks nice," I said.

"You look nice too. I assumed you must have been making up, that was why you were late. However, I do not see any makeup on your face," Cindy said teasingly.

"I overslept actually and thank you," I said, blushing.

"It is fine, I was just teasing you. So where are we going? you never gave me a name," Cindy said.

"You will love this place, fear not."

"Now you have gotten me excited," Cindy said as her face bubbled with excitement.

The restaurant I was taking Cindy to was the Golden Light restaurant, it was the best restaurant in the whole town and they served excellent cuisine from different parts of the world. This was why my parents used to take us there. It was the place to eat in town as they offered one of the best dining services. The feeling I got from going to the restaurant was second to none as there were always lovely scenes to observe around us.

The walls of the building were coated with gold paint and gave the whole restaurant a very classy look, the plants that were placed around the building often danced to the music in the room as their leaves moved from side to side. The marble tiles were always shiny and I always feared I was going to trip and fall one day, but that had still not happened yet. The customers there were always very friendly and quiet as if everyone was always trying to get lost in the music. The interior of the restaurant was also always visible from outside so it was easy to tell when the place was packed and perhaps turn back.

"Welcome to the Golden Light," someone at the door called out to Cindy and me as we made our way into the restaurant. A smiling employee showed us our table and told us that he would be our waiter for the day. He handed us a very classy-looking menu and told us he would be back to take our orders in a bit.

"This place is wonderful," Cindy announced and I could see how happy she was.

The soft music playing in the background made the whole atmosphere more relaxing and the aroma of the food from the couples sitting next to us teased our nostrils as we tried to make up our minds. The complimentary basket on our table was filled with mini snacks and I could see Cindy eye them on several occasions.

"What would you like to eat, please?" the waiter said as he appeared before us.

"I would like some green rice with the sauce, some

barbecue chicken breast, and a plate of your vegetable salad," I said as I closed my menu.

"I would like a plate of your Italian spaghetti and the sauce to go with it, no salad for me, please," Cindy said.

"What drinks would you like, please?"

"I think I will just have your freshly squeezed orange juice on the rocks."

"I think I will have the same thing he is having," Cindy said as the waiter noted down our order.

"I can't believe I did not know such a place existed. They have every type of food on their menu. Choosing a meal was very hard," Cindy announced.

"I had the same problem too the first time I came here. Things got better once I had tried a number of meals on their menu list."

"That must be nice. Do you guys come here a lot?" Cindy asked.

"Well, we used to; I have not come here since the death of my sister."

"I am so sorry. I hope you didn't have to choose this restaurant for me. I would hate to ruin your mood or be the reason why you are sad," Cindy said softly as she took my hands in hers. I had not allowed the memories that were shared in the restaurant with my sister to cloud my thoughts. Having Cindy there with me made everything better in a way I could not really explain.

To lighten the mood, she talked about her uncle and the embarrassing thing he had done on the first day of school. She also told me of how lost she had been when she had first come to Green Springs. She said she was shocked when she noticed that the school had its own coffee store in the cafeteria. She also told me of how she had entered the wrong class and sat in

Benny's seat. Benny was one of the mean girls in Green Springs and she was also the most popular girl. Her parents were also huge donors to the school and that automatically placed her on the popular hierarchy of the school's social strata. She used to date a guy on the football team and her cliques were hell-bent on going after every guy who played sports in the school.

By the time our food came, Cindy and I had laughed our eyes out, although silently as we did not want to be sent out. The green rice and sauce were amazing and the chicken breast was bursting with flavor as I ate it. Cindy had not been able to eat so much of her spaghetti as she had eaten the mini pastries in the complimentary baskets and was already half full before the food came. The drinks were spectacular as they had tried to maintain the freshness of the orange in the drink. I could taste the pulp with each sip. When we were both done with our food, I led Cindy to a place not too far from the restaurant. I was glad she had not worn heels because where we went to was a garden. The garden was where people often came to relax and hold picnics. It was a very large field and even had its own maze; however, I did not try the maze as I was scared that I was going to get lost.

"Okay, so this place is somewhere I have been to. I wonder how we missed the restaurant though," Cindy said as we both looked for a spot to sit in.

The garden was less crowded on that particular day and I was glad it was because I didn't really need an audience with what I was about to do. I had not been sure of the right time to tell her and when we finally found a good place to sit, we were both interrupted by my phone. I checked the caller ID and saw that it was from Kevin, I feared something had happened to Mr. Greg so I excused myself to answer the call.

"So?" Kevin said immediately I picked up the call.

"So what, Kevin?" I asked, confused.

"What did she say?" he asked.

"I have not yet asked her and you kind of interrupted what we were going to do."

"I told him not to bother you," I heard Paul shout from wherever he was.

"Cindy and Ken sitting on a tree KISSING," Kevin said as he made kissing noises over the phone.

"I am hanging up now, say hi to Mr. Greg for me," I said before ending the call, I knew if I continued talking to Kevin, he was probably never going to stop teasing me about kissing Cindy. I was all of a sudden scared as I walked back to where she was.

"Hi, sorry about that. It was Kevin on the phone," I said to Cindy.

"I hope nothing is wrong."

"Yeah, nothing is wrong. It is just Kevin being Kevin," I said.

"That is good to hear. Are you sure you are okay? You seem kind of off. Is something bothering you?" "Not really, I actually want to ask you a question," I said as I began to fidget. I was really nervous and I could tell Cindy noticed that too.

"Don't be nervous," she said as she held my hands.

"I wanted to know if you would like to be my girlfriend," I said in a rush.

Everywhere was silent for a while as I closed my eyes afraid of Cindy's reply. I could feel my heart pounding heavily in my chest as I patiently waited for her reply.

"Please open your eyes, Kendrick," Cindy said. I could feel her minty breath close to my face and when I opened my eyes, I saw her face close to mine.

"I would love to be your girlfriend," Cindy shouted and hugged me.

I became unable to move for a few seconds as I was still shocked by her reply. It felt unbelievable as I had expected her reply to be an absolute no, especially with my history.

"I am surprised you are just asking me now. I was already starting to think you were never going to do so and I felt I was going to do the asking out myself. You are a very special person to me, Ken, and you have brought a huge smile to my face ever since I met you," Cindy said, making me very emotional.

"I am so glad you said yes, Cindy. You have been one of the reasons why I find waking up very exciting. You are all I think about most times and I am more than grateful that you decided to come to Green Springs. You have been able to give my life more color, which I had assumed was forever gone. You just made me very happy, Cindy."

The first few moments felt like a dream to me as I was unable to comprehend the feelings that were running through my mind. It was one thing to be friends with someone and it was a completely different feeling when such a person decided to be your girlfriend. That day, as I dropped Cindy off at her house first, she pecked me lightly on my cheek and I felt myself floating. It was a wonderful experience.

CHAPTER TWENTY-THREE

The first day of senior year was one I could not forget. It was as if everyone had grown up during the summer as everyone looked taller and older in my eyes. Benny and her crew all wore matching uniforms, well except Benny who had done something different with hers. It felt great to be a senior because it was the finality of knowing that we had a few more months to spend in high school before finally going to college, although it was a bittersweet moment for me on the first day as I remembered Kevin and Christy would be traveling back to Europe immediately after high school. Kevin did not have perfect scores. His parents were going to help him pull some strings with the board of directors so he could go to Yale. Christy's parents were also doing this and although neither of them had any interest in going to Yale, they knew they could not defy their parents.

I had come to school in my new car, which I had gotten for my birthday after I had passed my driver's ed test. On the first day of school, I discovered that I needed coffee to function as I had spent all night studying in preparation for my SATs, which were still months away. However, I had not been able to drop my overplanning habit and so I stayed up all night planning my senior year. Although now that I remember that night, I wish I had just gone to bed instead of staying up at night as all my plans never became a reality.

As I stood in line for my coffee, two girls who I assumed were freshmen kept on looking at me and giggling at each other. They looked very shy and one of them looked like she wanted to talk to me. I grabbed a packet of sugar and poured some milk into my cup before my way was blocked by one of the girls again.

I kept wondering what they wanted from me as having girls hang around me was something I had experienced in the past whenever Cindy was not around. It was, however, still weird seeing it happen even when the entire school knew Cindy and I were an item.

"Hi, Ken," one of the girls said as she played with her hair funnily. "I am Sam's sister; he is on the school's swim team. I have seen you swim before." She said the last part like it was something she should be shy about.

"Oh, what is your name?" I asked her as I didn't know what to say. Her other friend just kept on looking at me in a way I found creepy.

"Laura," she said.

"Nice to meet you, Laura," I said as I tried to use my free hand to shake hers.

The bell soon rang and I could see how panicked the two girls looked. They looked like they were going to get punished if they got to class late and I could imagine the fear that must have been racing through their veins as I had experienced it too during my freshman days.

"You should get to class," I told them and I watched them scurry off, giggling to each other.

I had just begun to drink my coffee when I heard a loud

booming voice coming my way. I was able to predict who it was.

"SENIOR!" Kevin shouted as he made hooting noises in the cafeteria; some other senior responded and soon they were all sounding like monkeys that wanted to be free.

"Where is your senior spirit?' Kevin said as he threw his arm across my shoulders.

"It was in that coffee that I just drank," I answered quietly.

"I have a lot of things planned for us this year and I cannot wait to share it with you and the guys," Kevin said excitedly.

"I can't wait to hear it too," I said, trying to fake excitement. "Wait, why are we going in the same direction? Don't you have a class now too?"

"Well, we both have a class now. Together," Kevin said, emphasizing the last part.

"What have you done again this time?" I asked him.

"You know how this is going to be our last year together; I wanted to ensure I spent every moment with you," Kevin said as he batted his eyelashes at me like a girl.

"Should you not be saying this to your girlfriend and not me?" I asked him.

"Christy is going to be with me in college, so let me see other people now and she can have me all to herself when we are in Yale."

"I hope I am not the other people in that statement though," I asked, even though I already knew the answer.

"You know you are, Kennie," Kevin said, using the nickname I hated so much.

"I know you hate most of the classes I will be taking, so I don't know why you would want to torture yourself like this," I said.

"It's all for love," Kevin said with a smile that reached his eyes.

I grinned a bit as we walked to class, making a mental note to find out why my schedule was handed out to Kevin just like that.

My first class had been calculus and I knew how much Kevin hated anything that involved calculation. I knew he had sacrificed so much for me the previous year and I had suddenly found a way to repay him. I stopped in my tracks as we got to the door, making Kevin stumble and bump into me. "What did you stop for? Did you see people making out?" Kevin asked.

"No, I did not see people making out, Kevin; however, I have a better idea for how we could spend the first period," I said with a mischievous grin on my face.

"Wait, do you mean we should skip the first period?" he asked with wide eyes.

"Yes, that is exactly what I mean," I said to Kevin who looked at me like I had just offered him the entire earth.

"Who are you and what have you done to my best friend?" he asked, still shocked by what I had said.

"Do you still have the keys to the basketball court?" I asked Kevin, who was looking at me like I had grown some extra heads.

"Yes I still do, I picked them up immediately when I got to school," he said.

"That is perfect, let us go there." Dazed, Kevin just remained rooted to the spot. "Are you not coming with me?" I asked.

"You don't need to ask twice," Kevin said as we both took the shortcuts in the school building until we walked inside the basketball court.

The court was empty as expected and Kevin and I dropped our books and took a ball each. I was not ready to play against Kevin or share the same ball with him as he could get competitive when it came to playing basketball.

"So what college are you applying for?' he asked me as he threw a ball into the basket.

"Not sure yet, probably Brown or Cambridge."

"I can't believe we really won't be neighbors anymore, or even in the same country; I feel that is worse," Kevin said as he threw the basketball into the net in anger.

"We can still always meet up during the holidays," I suggested.

"I doubt my parents would allow me to leave the school premises at this rate, I might be forced to spend every waking moment in the walls of Yale."

"At least you have Christy," I said, trying to cheer him up, it was not every time I saw Kevin this down and I knew I had to try my best to make him happy.

"Christy is not you, Ken."

"I could also come and visit, I don't think my parents would be against that," I said.

"Really?" Kevin said as his eyes lit up.

"Yes," I said, smiling.

"Okay, now you deserve a bigger hug," Kevin said as he began to chase me around the court to hug me.

Kevin and I attended the next class just in time before the bell rang, we were lucky not to have gotten caught as it would have been on our permanent record and would probably have ruined the record I had been trying to set as a straight-A student. The day rolled by so fast and soon enough it was time for lunch, the whole cafeteria was full by the time we got there but that had never been a problem for us. As seniors who played sports, we also had a lot of privileges. We had our table where it was just us, seniors, alone; this table was grouped into five and various cliques sat down on it according to their category. On my table, it was just Tee, Becky, Kevin, Paul, and I who sat down there. Tee had been able to order our special table and the table had been shipped in before we resumed school.

We had also gotten a lot of special treatment because of Tee's parents who had requested that Tee had his chef brought into school since Tee was a vegetarian. Being friends with Tee had its privileges and this was one that every one of us had been looking forward to all through our winter break. Kevin had dashed out of the class immediately the bell rang, not like he had been listening to what the teacher had been saying previously though. He tried to decide what he would ask the chef to make in a few minutes so he would have enough time to enjoy his lunch.

"Hey Tee, where are Becky and Paul?" I asked, greeting everyone in general as I took my seat.

"Tee, where is your chef?" Kevin asked, interrupting me as he looked around the hall like a starved animal.

"He does not resume work today sadly," Tee said with a smile.

"What, you mean I will have to eat the cafeteria food today? Do you know how long I have dreamt of this?" Kevin wailed.

"He has been planning," I chirped in, just to show them the seriousness of Kevin's situation.

"I already ordered us something to eat," Tee informed Kevin.

"Really, so where is it?' Kevin asked as he looked at the empty table.

"There," Tee said pointing towards Becky and Paul who were carrying two paper bags each in their hands.

"Oh, I love you guys," Kevin declared loudly as Paul and Becky took their seats.

Tee had ordered a vegetable salad and energy drinks for himself while he had ordered burgers, fries, chicken, chocolate, and milkshake for all of us. It was always a shock to me whenever Tee ordered such meals for us, especially since he was a vegetarian. I had asked him previously in the past if our eating animals did not disturb him and he shrugged and told me he did not mind as long as he was not the one eating them. According to Tee, we were only killing ourselves with those unhealthy foods and he was sure we were all going to die before him; little did he know how incorrect he was.

"So guys, I have come up with a great plan," Kevin said as he continued to stuff food in his mouth.

"Let us hear it," Paul said as he gingerly sipped his milkshake.

"I have planned a trip for us this weekend to a cabin. I saw this place online and I was able to book us a reservation there before it got filled up. They also have a park there and an escape room so I know it will be fun. You all must come as this is just one out of the many trips I have planned for us before the end of our senior year," Kevin said happily as ketchup dropped from his chin.

"Did you do proper research for this place? I am sure everyone still remembers how you got us lost in eighth grade," Becky said.

"That was centuries ago. I am surprised you still remember such a thing," Kevin said, looking annoyed.

"If that is the case then I am in," Becky said.

"Me too," said Tee.

"Same here," Paul said as he picked up a fry before dipping it in a pool of ketchup.

All eyes turned to stare at me as I remained the only one who had not said anything.

"I doubt if I will be able to make it; I promised Cindy I would take her out this weekend, especially since she just got back from California and I haven't seen her all through winter," I said.

"Invite her on the trip then, we all like her and she spends a considerable amount of time with us already so this would not be a big deal," Kevin said and the other guys nodded their heads in agreement.

"But don't you think she would feel weird being the only girl there? I think you should invite Christy to balance the equation," I said.

"If I invited Christy, Becky would also want to invite his girlfriend and Tee would want to bring his dog," Kevin said.

"No, we do not!" Becky and Tee said simultaneously.

"Okay, I will text her and see if she would like to come. Does that mean the trip is confirmed?" Kevin said as he squealed like a girl.

"Yes," we all chorused as Kevin tried to make us high-five him with his sticky fingers.

Thursday came by so fast and Tee was to welcome to our school some golf celebrities, who I had been unable to identify until they showed me their pictures. We therefore had to help him pick up his suit from the store. We had also been given a permission slip to follow Tee to the suit store and leave school as long as we all participated in the event. We had all agreed to help him out so we were more than happy to slip out of school before the bell rang.

The store where Tee was to get his suit from was one of

those fancy stores that not just anyone could walk into. The whole interior screamed of money and I was scared to touch anything.

"Welcome, sir," the shop attendant said immediately we walked in.

The song Ave Maria blasted from the speaker as we were handed little champagne flutes. I was tempted to ask if they were aware that none of us were eighteen yet, but I had instead swallowed my questions as I saw the others drink theirs.

It turned out to be just a fruit punch that was served in a fancy glass.

"I don't think you can just pick any one you like and wear it," I said, horrified at Kevin, who was going through the endless suit racks and testing them out.

"You should stop before the owner of the store finds you doing so. I doubt your mother would be willing to bail you out from this one," Paul said.

That seemed to strike a nerve as Kevin flinched; in a matter of seconds, however, he had his smiling face back on again.

"Do you need any help over here, sir?" A smiling saleslady who looked like she would prefer to be anywhere but in the store came to stand by us.

"No assistance is needed here," Paul said as he stood up straighter. It was something he often did unconsciously and was meant to make him look older.

"Okay, call me if you need anything. I will be standing over there," she said, pointing to a corner.

After a few minutes had gone by, Tee came out of the dressing room with a lot of bags making me wonder why he needed so many suits.

"Guys, I have asked Antonio here to arrange a suit here

for you and he has been able to do so on such quick notice," Tee said, like buying a suit for your friends was something people just did out of the blue.

We all stood there in the middle of the store shocked as to what was happening before Antonio called our names one by one and took us to the dressing room to ensure that the suit he handed to us was a perfect size. Before we left the store, we all ended up carrying shopping bags as we drove to school. It had been one of those moments when Tee left us silent. Even Kevin remained quiet on the drive back home.

When I got home, I changed into a pair of sport shorts and stretched out on a pool chair in the backyard. The cushion was dusty, and as I listened to the water lap against the landscaped rocks that made up our fake waterfall I tried to remember the last time I had sat on this particular chair. It was the chair my sister had been able to crawl out from, which led to her death. I did not know how I felt about sitting in it at that moment, but I was aware that sitting in it was a big step for me. It was like I was ready to admit that Star was never coming back and I was no longer alone now that I had Cindy. The sun was hot on my chest and so bright that I could barely read the handwriting in my German exercise book. I had taken German as an extra credit course for reasons still unknown to me to date. I felt like I was about to go blind from the way the sun was shining on me.

"Ken, what are you doing?" my mom shrilled, startling me.

I rolled over and squinted toward the house, where she hovered behind the screen door, carrying a plate of cookies.

"I was studying," I called back.

"What were you thinking? You could have gotten yourself blind," Mom said gently as I joined her behind the screen door. She was still in her apron, which made her look more tired.

"You should not be stressing yourself," I said to her as I took a bite out of one of the cookies. "Wow, these are amazing," I said as I stuffed more into my mouth.

"Thank you, I actually came out to let you know that Cindy is around," my mother said as she walked into the kitchen to continue what she was doing.

"Mother! Why did you not start with that?" I said, alarmed.

"Well, you almost made yourself go blind and that distracted me," my mother said as she shrugged her shoulders.

"How long has she been here?" I asked.

"Well, a few minutes actually. I told her to make herself comfortable in your room."

"Thanks, Mother," I said as I ran upstairs towards my room.

"Hi girlfriend," I said as I gave Cindy a huge peck on her cheek.

"Why is your body so hot?" Cindy asked with wide eyes.

"Probably the heavy lifting I do," I said cheekily.

"Oh please, you know I was not talking about that," Cindy said, blushing.

"Really? I had no clue," I said as I settled down on the bed with her and increased the air conditioning in the room.

"Why do you do this?" Cindy said as she covered her beautiful smile with her hands.

"Turned you into a blushing bride," I said as I found her ticklish spot and began to tickle her.

"NOOOO, PLEASE STOP!" Cindy shouted as she busted out laughing. "I think I am going to pee, please

Kendrick," she said as tears began to form in her eyes from laughing too much.

"I'm only stopping because I do not want you peeing on my hot body, I don't want you to find me unattractive just yet," I said as I hugged her tightly to my chest.

"My payback would be sweeter," Cindy announced as she rested properly on my shoulders.

"Dream on, sweets," I said as I stroked her hair.

"So are you guys all set for tomorrow?" Cindy asked.

"Yes we are, Tee is renting an RV just in case the place Kevin picked out for us is no good. We will be coming to pick you up in that," I said.

"I am so excited, are you sure the guys are cool with me tagging along? I do not want to ruin this trip for you boys," Cindy said.

"They were the ones who actually suggested you come along and also Christy is coming along too so you have nothing to worry about."

"I can't wait for tomorrow."

"Same here, this trip already promises to be fun," I said, jinxing the whole trip before it even started.

"Would you like to watch a movie?" I asked.

"Yes," Cindy said like she had been waiting for the question all day.

"Okay, which one?" I asked, curious all of a sudden.

"I brought one with me," she announced.

"Why do I have a feeling it is going to be something romantic?"

"Well, you guessed right, babe," Cindy said as she pulled out a *Lady and the Tramp* DVD from her bag.

"But we have seen that together already," I wailed.

"It never gets old and that is what I would like to watch,

or would you deny your girlfriend that privilege?" Cindy said, pouting in a way that made her so adorable.

"You win, *Lady and the Tramp* it is," I said, giving up.

"Are you going to get me some of those cookies you were eating?" Cindy asked.

"What, how could you tell? I already finished it before coming upstairs," I asked, shocked.

"A detective never reveals his secret," Cindy said before taking a bow.

"That is not how the saying goes," I said, smiling as I made my way downstairs to the kitchen.

The rest of the day was spent reciting lines from our favorite movies and doing funny accents. It was a day I wished I had been able to prolong.

CHAPTER TWENTY-FOUR

The RV Tee had rented was so cool, it basically had all of the facilities of a real home and it was stocked with everything. When Cindy saw it, her mouth was left hanging and she had the same reaction I had as the boys teased us all the way. The road trip was a lot of fun even though Kevin peed like a thousand times, denying everyone access to the bathroom since he was always in it. We all shared jokes and laughed together as we made fun of things we saw on the street. It was one of the best road trips ever.

"Did you hear me okay?" I asked Cindy as I noticed that she had zoned out on me without actually knowing it.

"I am so sorry, what did you say? I was lost in the beautiful sight in front of us; I do not think I have seen so many butterflies gathered in one particular place before," Cindy said in awe as she turned to face me.

"I just confirmed our sleeping arrangements from Kevin; we are going to have to share a room. I hope that is alright with you, he said there are no empty rooms and Christy is already sharing a room with him," I said, rambling on shyly.

"This will be our first time spending the night together, it is something I have always wanted," Cindy said as she blushed.

"Can someone get these two love birds to their room already?" Paul said teasingly.

"Christy, you can see I can play cupid very well. Never doubt my skills," Kevin said, addressing Christy who just rolled her eyes at him before giving Cindy a thumbs up.

"Kendrick and Cindy sitting on a tree K.I.S.S.I.N.G." Becky began to sing.

"I did not mean it that way, guys," Cindy said as she realized how my friends must have interpreted her statement.

"Cindy, don't you go turning all shy with us. It is okay to talk about these things. This is a safe space," Paul said, laughing. Paul had been very cool since the beginning of the trip and it was something we didn't get to see all the time. In school, he was even more reserved than I was and only talked whenever he was with us, his friends.

"Paul, please stop," Cindy said as she blushed even harder, making everyone laugh all the more.

"You guys, leave her alone," I said as I tried to take her hands in mine.

We arrived at our destination in no time, the place was breathtaking and everyone patted Kevin on the back for doing a good job. We all went to our separate rooms and I helped Cindy carry her luggage to our room. The room Kevin picked for us was a master room. It had a wonderful king-sized bed and a large mirror that you could fit a whole country in and still see it.

There was a mini-fridge, which had snacks, and some cups were neatly arranged in it. There was also a pull-out sofa in the left corner of the room with a huge seventy-two-inch plasma television hanging above it. There was a large wardrobe that could take everyone's clothes if they wanted to keep them in our room.

"Okay, I have to admit that Kevin outdid himself here," I said as I continued to inspect the room.

"I am still in awe and I feel like I have just walked into a whole new world," Cindy said as she also looked very impressed by all that she was seeing.

"Honestly, I am so happy I was invited on this trip. I cannot even imagine what I would have been doing today if I had missed out on all the fun that Kevin has promised us this weekend."

"I heard we will be going to the park tomorrow and might even camp outside if the weather permits it," I said excitedly. I had never been camping before at that point and it was something I had looked forward to in all the activities that Kevin had planned.

"Should we discuss sleeping arrangements?" Cindy asked out of the blue as her face heated up.

"Sure, do you want me to sleep somewhere else?" I asked, walking towards the pull-out sofa.

"No, I did not mean I want you to sleep somewhere else, what I want to know is if you slept on your right side or your left side," Cindy said.

"Is there a difference?" I asked, shocked that people considered things like that.

"Yes, there is."

"Oh, please educate me. Which do you prefer?"

"I sleep on the left side," Cindy said.

"You know you have to explain more if you want to sleep on that right side."

"I said left side," Cindy said, correcting me.

"Sorry, your highness, please tell me why the LEFT SIDE?"

"I read in a book that people who sleep on the left side

are less likely to get murdered or start their day in a crappy mood than people who sleep on the right," Cindy said with a straight face.

I immediately burst out laughing until I saw the seriousness on her face and realized that she was not joking.

"Wait, you are serious about this?"

"Yes, I am, and stop laughing," Cindy said as she pouted and crossed her arms.

"Hold up, so you would rather I get murdered," I said as the realization of what she said finally dawned on me.

"You said you don't believe so I do not understand what you are saying at the moment," Cindy said, trying to play smart.

"My girlfriend doesn't like me," I said as I tried to be very dramatic.

"You are not serious. I am still sleeping on the left," Cindy said as she looked me squarely in the eye.

"Yes ma'am, your wish is my command," I said, bowing to her like a gentleman.

I reached for my phone next to check a notification I had just received and noticed that it was from Becky telling us to hurry down.

"Sweets, we need to hurry down now as Kevin is in a food war and is planning on devouring our food if we do not go down immediately," I said.

"Kevin and food though. Let us go now and save our hungry stomachs. To infinity and beyond. Also, you need to tell me the secret of Kevin's stomach, I need to know how he eats that much and still stays fit," Cindy said as we headed towards the door of our room.

I was unable to hold back my smile as we walked downstairs because I was too happy. Being with Cindy made my heart flutter and also gave me a sense of purpose.

"Look who decided to join us," Paul said as Cindy and I walked down the stairs.

"It was not like you waited for us," Cindy said to Paul while pointing at his already half-eaten food.

"I did not know how long it was going to take you guys to finish what you started in the RV," Paul said teasingly.

"Paul, drop it," I said when I saw Cindy turn red all over.

Dinner was wonderful as we all talked about our favorite things in life. As we talked, Tee stood up abruptly in a way we all found strange. After about ten minutes he came back with a huge box that was bigger than him. I was still surprised that he had been able to carry it when he spoke.

"I am sure you all are wondering what is inside this box," Tee said mischievously.

"Is there any cash reward if my answer is no?" Becky asked.

"No Becky, and stop interrupting me," Tee said as he rolled his eyes at him.

"Hey, that was only a suggestion. Do not shoot the messenger, please," Becky cried out.

"Now, back to what I was saying. I would like all of you to guess what is inside this box and the winner will get to keep what is inside for the night."

"You brought your chef here," Kevin said eagerly.

"Kevin, how could he put him inside the box?" Paul asked as he eyed Kevin.

"The box is large and anything is possible with Tee," Kevin stated in his own defense.

"Next person, please," Tee said as he looked around the room.

"iPhones for all of us," Becky said.

"Seriously Becky, what is your obsession with changing phones all the time? Did you not just get a new phone just last week?" Kevin asked.

"It was a guess, you don't have to get your boxers all worked up," Becky said as he stuck his tongue out childishly.

"You guys should take this seriously," Tee said as he drummed his fingernails on the box.

"Is it something that can break?" Paul asked Tee.

"We did not get clues, so we see no reason why you should," Becky said.

"No one asked you not to ask for clues though, so just count it as your loss," Paul said, smiling.

"There is no clue Paul, so please just guess already," Tee said. It looked like his patience had been worn thin already.

"Shoes," Christy said, trying to ease the tension.

"Not shoes," Tee answered, smiling now.

"Books," Cindy supplied.

"Wrong also," Tee said.

"Tickets to see a famous celebrity," Paul said.

This made everyone laugh. It sounded strange that he would even think Tee would put tickets in a very large box.

However, as I was about to answer, the box started moving and this was when everyone began guessing moving objects.

"It's a remote-controlled car," I said.

"A plane."

"A mouse."

Tee just rolled his eyes at all of our suggestions and decided that he had heard enough and was ready to talk.

"So, what you could not guess correctly was..." Tee said as he unwrapped the box slowly, while whatever was in it made the box dance.

"Brown!" Tee said as his dog jumped out of the box.

"It was your dog all along?" Paul shouted.

"I can't believe I overworked my brain for this," Kevin said, making everybody look at him weirdly.

"You have finally named your dog," I said when everybody had finally quieted down and Brown lay on the floor wagging his tail.

"Yes, I realized the name had been on his body all along," Tee said with a smile.

"Really, where?" Becky said as he got up from the chair to inspect Brown's body.

"I didn't mean a name was written on his body already, silly; the spots on his body are brown so that automatically makes him Brown," Tee said proudly.

"I cannot believe you, Tee," Paul said, groaning while we all laughed.

The night flew by fast and we all said our goodnights as we made our way to our different rooms.

"Do not try anything I would not do," Kevin called out to me as I led Cindy to the room.

"I believe the right phrase is 'Do not do anything he would do or not do' actually," Paul said, chuckling as he disappeared into the darkness.

"That was creepy," Cindy said as she looked to where Paul had disappeared into. She and Christy had gone into Kevin's room earlier to talk for a minute and I was curious to know what they had said.

"Paul can be that way sometimes," I said as I held the room door open for her.

"It is amusing seeing this side of him, it still shocks me," Cindy admitted.

"Do not worry; you will get used to it soon," I said. "So,

what were you and Christy talking about?" I asked, letting my curiosity get the best of me.

"Nothing you should know about, just girl talk," Cindy said, winking at me.

"Okay then, I shall ask no more. Are you ready to take a shower yet?" I asked her.

"Yes, although I must warn you I spend up to three hours in the bathroom," Cindy said with a straight face.

"I am joking," she said, laughing as she saw the shock on my face. "I will be out in no time."

That night, Cindy and I cuddled together as we drifted off to sleep; it was a wonderful sleep and I hugged her tight as I promised never to let her go. Little did I know that I was making a promise I could never keep.

The next morning was one I wish I had never got to experience whenever I think about this day and see the signs I missed. It was as if the universe had been trying to tell me something that I had ignored on countless occasions. I had woken up to see Cindy groaning and I immediately began to panic, thinking the worst had happened. She instructed me to help her get her medicine from her bag and I did so in haste, stumbling over the rug in the center of our room. I held her up so she could sit properly and I was tempted to call Christy into the room in case she needed a feminine presence. After a few minutes went by and she looked like she had fully recovered as she could now talk.

"You learned sign language so fast," Cindy said teasingly.

"Were those hand movements sign language?" I asked, surprised because I didn't know she knew sign language.

"No, I was just teasing you," Cindy said as she patted the bed for me to come and sit down.

I had not realized I had been pacing around the room,

I had felt very helpless and scared. I was glad I could finally relax.

"It must have been the food I ate yesterday. I must have eaten more than my stomach could handle," Cindy said as she rested her head on my shoulders.

"I thought it was cramp," I admitted with a blush. "You know you do not have to go anywhere today, right? We can just sit here in the hotel and watch movies all day."

"You want me to miss all the fun? I am going!" Cindy said excitedly as she pecked my cheeks.

I smiled at her before kissing her on the lips. She looked so beautiful that I felt like the luckiest man on the planet. She returned my kiss and my fingers found their way to her hair. Pulling her down as I lowered her to lie flat on her back, my heart felt like it was going to explode as pleasure swept through my body like a wave without control; I had to chant in my head to control myself as my gaze swept over her body. My fingers trailed all over her body and I saw her shake under my touch. I showered soft kisses all over her neck and she pressed her body closer to mine, which only drove me crazy. I was about to lose the little voice of reasoning I had left in my body when the door to our room made a loud sound indicating that someone was coming in.

I quickly rolled off Cindy and allowed her to adjust her dress. I knew I was going to kill whoever had interrupted us and I had an idea of who it might be even before he walked inside.

"I have been calling you non-stop, why have you not been picking up?" Kevin said as he made his way to our bed. "Oops, I didn't know you were busy," he added as he saw the murderous gaze I was sending his way as he looked between me and Cindy.

"What do you want, Kevin?" I asked, trying to calm my anger down. Kevin was about to talk when Christy entered the room looking embarrassed on his behalf.

"I told him not to come in," Christy said as she looked at Kevin like he was a little child.

"What I wanted to say was very urgent and I was also worried when you failed to pick up," Kevin said as he tried to justify his interruption.

"What was so important, Kevin?" I asked, still sounding angry so he would know he was not off the hook yet.

"I wanted to let you know that the time for the haunted house show has been shifted and we now have to go this morning," he said, making a very funny facial expression to show his seriousness.

"Thanks, Kevin," Cindy said as she smiled at him.

"You see, Christy, Cindy understands," Kevin announced to Christy happily.

"Let's just go, I am sure they need to get back to what they were doing before you rudely interrupted them," Christy said as she sent a wink to Cindy, which only made her blush.

"Don't spend too much time here. We leave in a few minutes," Kevin said as he looked at me smiling.

I escorted them back to the door and ensured I locked the door behind me this time; I had forgotten to do so the previous night and regretted that my forgetfulness had cost us a special moment. I walked towards the bed and saw Cindy in her towel, I groaned quietly as I walked towards her.

"Don't tell me you want to take your shower now," I said, looking very hurt as I drew her into my embrace.

"I do," Cindy said, chuckling.

"You may now kiss the groom," I said teasingly, hoping she got the joke.

"Oh my, you didn't ask if I could marry you," Cindy said in between fits of laughter. "I meant I do, to take a shower."

"You just broke my heart," I said as I placed my hands on my chest.

"I would, however, still like to kiss you," Cindy said shyly.

I did not wait for her to do so and I kissed her instead. I felt my lips curve into a smile as I realized how happy kissing her made me feel. She broke off the kiss and scurried away into the bathroom. I laughed as I realized that she had her moments of shyness. At that point, I knew there was nothing I would not want to do for her.

Getting ready did not take as much time as I had thought it would and Cindy went ahead to Christy's room before I had come out of the bathroom. I tried to convince her to allow us to stay back in the hotel, but she was bent on us joining everyone to avoid missing out on the fun. I knew I would rather spend more time with her than the boys since I had known all of them longer than I had known her. Kevin tried to apologize when he saw me downstairs, he promised to get me a sneaker signed by one of our favorite NBA stars just to make up for his sins. I tried to keep a straight face when he had said this because I knew I had already forgiven him. However, I didn't let him know this as getting those signed sneakers had always been one of my desires. We all trooped into the RV as we headed towards our first destination. No one had been interested in breakfast except Kevin and he munched a double cheeseburger on the way. Watching him eat it was a sight to behold as he gave the burger his utmost concentration. The haunted house was located in a street with a very narrow road; I still think Kevin and Christy started holding each other's hand right from there. The house was covered by so many tall trees and I wondered who could have taken their time to plant that number of trees. When we finally got to the house, I was surprised when I saw the building. The building looked historic, like something I had seen in one of my history books. The bricks on the walls looked like they had chipped off and Paul believed that the holes we had seen in the wall on our way to the entrance were bullet holes.

"Welcome to funders filed haunted house. Beware of the zombies. Please kindly drop your phones into this bag," a chirpy tour guide said as she stood beside us and waited for us to drop our phones into the bag.

"Were those bullet holes on the walls at the entrance?" Kevin asked, looking very concerned.

"Yes, they were," the woman said, offering no further explanation as she handed us guns and kept our phones in a safe.

"Do we get to shoot these?" Tee asked excitedly.

"Yes, you do. If you do not, you will die," the lady said, smiling as if she had just announced we were going to get free doughnuts. Cindy walked closer to me with her gun held tightly towards her and I smiled as she slid her hands in mine.

"You all have a required number of bullets in your guns, so please avoid wasting them on things that do not require you to shoot at them," the woman said as she continued to lead us into a place that now looked like a tunnel; I could barely see anymore and I began to get scared too, although I couldn't let that show because of Cindy.

"I will leave you here now," the woman said as she pressed a button and the tunnel was illuminated by a red light.

"How do we find our way out of here?" Becky and Paul asked simultaneously.

"It's the last door you will see," the woman said as she began to walk away.

"Whose idea was it for us to come here?" Kevin asked as he looked like he would rather be anywhere else.

"Yours," we all chorused.

"Let's just go and see if we are lucky enough to find our way out," Becky said.

We all walked together and at the same pace since no one wanted to get left behind. There were cobwebs everywhere and some of them got into Cindy's and Christy's hair. We walked for a few minutes and discovered there was nothing really scary about the place. It looked like your normal haunted Halloween house with the ghosts that jump out in front of you and the fake spiders. We had all begun to talk freely among ourselves, no longer afraid of the building, until we began to hear strange noises. It sounded like people were screaming in pain and the sound became deafening as we neared a certain door with "Exit" written on it. We were all happy thinking we were safe when we saw that we had entered a room filled with tombs. The tombs were all arranged on the wall and, as we passed, they shook vigorously. I already began to fear what was in the tombs and Tee advised everyone to get their guns ready. He had been the only one looking excited at the prospect of shooting things. As we readied our guns, we heard a sudden ripping sound that sounded like a cloth was being torn. The moment this sound was heard, the tombs began to open of their own accord and zombies and mummies began to march forward. At first, no one believed they were real until Tee shot one of them and blood splashed all over our bodies. No one stopped to check if the blood was real or not as we all began to run for our dear lives. We were all screaming like little girls as we ran, Tee had to remind us to use our guns since he was the only one shooting at the zombies.

CHAPTER TWENTY-FIVE

As soon as we began shooting, more zombies came out as if they had been waiting for the sound of the guns. We were outnumbered and I replayed the words of the interesting tour guide and could only hope we were not going to die. I held on to Cindy's hand as we ran and shot the zombies together. Tee was able to shoot a large number of the zombies and mummies and soon we were stuck in front of a door that read, "More Danger, Keep Away." We all looked at each other as we tried to weigh our options. We knew if we stayed outside, we were going to get killed by the zombies. However, if we entered despite the huge warning sign we had just read, we were not sure of what danger might lie ahead waiting for us. Kevin suggested we do rock, paper, scissors for it, but we did not have that luxury because the zombies, who were meant to be walking slowly, now seemed to have gotten faster as they advanced towards us. No one thought twice before rushing through the door, it took us a few minutes to realize we were now outside. The tour lady had explained to us that the signs on the doors were only written to distract and confuse us. The exit sign had been written there to lure us inside while the danger sign had been placed there so people would spend more time inside and they could make more money due to how scared people often were.

"Please come back again," the tour lady said as she waved at us.

"We won't be doing so," Kevin said, still annoyed since we were all making fun of him for screaming the loudest.

Our next stop was a carnival; I was shocked when I discovered how large the event was. People had gathered from all over the world to celebrate nothing in particular and just have fun. It seemed ridiculous at that point, but I am now grateful that I got to participate in it. The whole group seemed more relaxed when we discovered Kevin had not planned another scary adventure for us. We all broke apart as we decided to meet back at the RV once it was five o'clock. There were a lot of rides to go on and Cindy looked like she wanted to try every one. I knew it was my duty as her boyfriend to win her a stuffed animal and I scanned the carnival looking for a game I could play and win one for her. She insisted we rode on a roller coaster first and I was scared to admit I was afraid of roller coasters. I looked up and saw people screaming like guns were pointed to their heads and my fear only worsened.

Cindy took my hands in hers as if sensing my fear and gave me a quick kiss on the cheek.

"We don't have to get on this ride," she said. I could tell from the way she had smiled at the roller coaster the moment we got down from the RV that she must like roller coasters and I knew I was not going to deny her the pleasure of going on one.

"Never been on one, so I don't think you would want to deny me experiencing this with you," I said reassuringly so she couldn't see through my act.

"I wouldn't want to do that," Cindy said as she pulled me

to the ticket booth. We met Kevin and Christy who wanted us to come and stand in front of them; Cindy and I were, however, not interested in cutting the line. The line was not so long and we believed waiting in line was better since we were less likely to get insulted that way.

It wasn't long before it became time for us to take our seat on the ride, Cindy ensured we both sat safely and held my hands. The moment I felt the ride start to move my eyes closed shut on impulse. My heart started beating faster and I resisted the urge to scream and jump down from whatever point we had gotten to. I could hear Cindy chuckling beside me and I looked at her and smiled. Seeing the lovely smile on her face was enough to make my fears disappear. I discovered the ride was not as scary as I had imagined it to be and I found myself enjoying the adrenaline rush that came with being on such a ride.

Once the ride was over we both ordered hot dogs and ice cream, we found a quiet place to eat and Cindy told me more about her childhood. She sounded very happy when she talked to me and I was glad she was able to embrace the sad part of her childhood. It was something I had promised to do on my part too. We played a paintball game next when we caught up with the group at the paintball arena. It was filled with so much laughter. Tee and Becky had both teamed up and deceived everyone into thinking they belonged to different teams. They both attacked every one of us and only stopped when they noticed we were all covered in paint from our heads to our toes. Kevin promised to avenge us and it was a hilarious decision as he sounded prehistoric when he said it.

I played a game of hitting the bottles. I had to play the game three times before I was able to win a stuffed animal, I felt Cindy deserved it. We both walked back to the RV hand in hand, not before stealing a kiss behind the RV. I believed at that point that it was the most perfect day ever. The drive back to our final destination was fun; my friends told Cindy a lot of embarrassing stories about me. I was almost the same color as a tomato by the time we got to the lake.

The scene before us when we got to the lake was breathtaking. The water in the lake looked like it had been painted silver, the reflection of the sun made it look more inviting. The quietness around us was deafening as the movement of the trees became the only thing we could hear. It felt like a place you would want to retire to; we all stood for a few minutes in silence as we gazed upon the beautiful scenery before us.

"How did you find this place?" Christy asked as she stared at Kevin like she was seeing him in a new light.

"My grandfather owns it," Kevin said proudly. It was one of the few times I had seen him brag about anything he owned. "Come on, let me take you to your rooms," he said.

"What about our bags? I didn't know we were sleeping here," Paul said, complaining.

"I sent a text message to everyone this morning. I also took the liberty of transferring all our luggage down here," Kevin said.

"Thanks, but I hope you didn't go through my stuff?" Paul asked curiously.

"You have a nice hair conditioner, I already ordered something similar so we can both have the same hair texture," Kevin said before glancing at Paul and running into the lake house. Paul wasted no time in chasing Kevin; we all knew their cat and mouse chase might take a while and so we decided to take a tour of the lake house by ourselves. The cabin was beautifully designed, it was also very modern and had a lot of gadgets that I had never set my eyes on before. There was no chair, but there were bean bags around, which we all sat on. Cindy and I sat on one and I held her close so she could lie on my shoulders. After a few minutes, Kevin came back to where we were all seated and offered to show us our room. Cindy and I got a very good room again and I was starting to wonder if Kevin was giving us the good rooms on purpose. There was a bed inside a bamboo bed frame, it looked unique and I allowed my hands to get a good feel of the bamboo to be sure it was real. The bathroom was covered in mirrors and we had a fireplace with real fire. I felt at peace there and I realized I had not thought of my sister all through the trip.

"I found marshmallows!" Cindy announced as she brought me back to the present.

"Should we eat them now?" I asked as I looked at her smiling face.

"It says on the note that we have to wait until evening to eat them," Cindy said as she read the note attached to it.

"I don't think anyone will notice if we take some out of it and seal it back up," I suggested to her.

"Do you have a sealing machine in that small bag you brought?" Cindy asked teasingly.

"Why did you have to bring my bag into this?" I said, pouting.

"You packed so little; I find it hard not to be jealous."

"I could teach you how to pack like this," I said as I hugged Cindy. Hugging her was something I enjoyed doing.

We both decided to take a short nap before going outside to join our friends. Our short nap lasted for an hour and I was awakened by a loud banging noise on our door.

"Go away," I shouted as I watched Cindy rub her sleepy eyes before going to open the door.

"The game is about to start; do not shoot the messenger," Tee said as he looked at my sleeping form.

"Thanks, Tee," I called out to him as he made his way out of the room. I had forgotten I had promised to watch the game with the guys. We all watched the same sports despite not being good at them. I had been watching basketball with Kevin ever since I discovered he was good at it. It had been a ritual among all of us to ensure that we understood each other's sports interests and also find ways to help ourselves grow.

"Christy just texted me, she wants us to relax by the lake and talk," Cindy said as she continued to rub her eyes gently. She looked so cute and I was tempted to kiss her.

"I could come and join you there once the game is over," I said as I walked towards her and hugged her again.

"That would be nice," Cindy said as she snuggled into my arms.

It was a picture of a perfect moment I should have gotten on camera. I stole one last kiss from Cindy before going to watch the game with my friends. It was a basketball game and Kevin often turned games like this into an argument. I took my seat by the window so I could look at Cindy whenever I wanted to; Kevin, however, felt I was not paying attention when he asked for my opinion about a player and I could not answer. He swapped my seat with his and I discovered I could no longer see Cindy. I went out to give her a diet Cooke and told her and Christy a funny story about Kevin's basketball arguments. I went back inside the house smiling as I continued the game.

Once the game was over the boys and I went over each player's mistake and applauded the winning team for playing extraordinarily well that night. We all then decided to join the girls at the lake and also joked about swimming in the lake. Tee was in the process of betting one of his signed shirts by Tiger Woods when I suddenly felt a chill. I felt as if the air had been knocked out of my lungs, and I ran towards the lake sensing danger.

I stopped frozen to the spot when I saw the scene playing out in front of me—I could see my friends jumping into the lake trying to save the two drowning ladies. I had still not moved when the ambulance arrived and the next time I woke up it was in a hospital again.

The first thing I heard when I woke up was the distant voice of my friends. The noise in my head did not allow me to make sense of what it was exactly they wanted to tell me. I tried opening my mouth to find out what was going on, but no sound came out of my mouth. I drifted in and out of consciousness throughout the day and I briefly caught a glimpse of people as they came in and out of my room. I had no memory of what had happened and so I had wondered why I was in the hospital.

CHAPTER TWENTY-SIX

The smell of bacon and eggs woke me up, I felt I was hungry right from my dream, and my mouth salivated in anticipation of food. I rolled to my side and gently opened my eyes; I saw my friends gathered around my bed. They all looked like they had been crying and had not slept in days; what was weirder was seeing Tee look very unkempt. Tee always loved dressing up; he was the most stylish person among us. There was a certain day when he forgot to brush his hair and had come to school that way. When he discovered this, he had looked so alarmed that one would have thought he had seen a ghost. He faked an emergency and was allowed to go back home. He had come back with perfectly styled hair. That day had been full of laughter. Those were the things that were missing from my friends' eyes. Tee was wearing a very big white shirt and jeans. It was very unlike him not to have a sweater or a muffler draped around his neck. He explained his reason for wearing them to people by saying he was always cold. This was not true, however, as he had once told us that he only wore it to look classy and also pair his clothes together.

"What is going on?" I was confused as to why I was wearing an oxygen mask or needed one.

"You don't remember?" Kevin said, looking shocked, and I shook my head in the negative.

Kevin remained silent and looked at the others. They were about to open their mouths and talk when my parents walked in. My mother looked at me for a long time like she could not believe my eyes were open. She called for the doctor and my friends were asked to wait in the hallway while I was examined again. The doctor promised that I was going to get my memory back as long as I did not overwork my brain. I still felt very confused as he talked; I wondered what I had forgotten. When the doctor left, my mother ran to me and hugged me. She kept saying I would be fine so many times that I was forced to wonder if she was trying to convince herself or me. I drifted off shortly, still confused; I knew something important was missing, but I just didn't know what it was.

The next time I woke up, I was in my bed in my room. The familiar setting of my room gave me joy as I became glad that I was no longer in the hospital. I found the strength to stand up from my bed and walk around my room. I don't know why I felt walking around my room was important at that point; I am glad I did so now though. As I walked around I tried to jog my memory so I could understand what had been so terrible that I had tried to forget. I paced around slowly for a few minutes and was still unable to come up with an answer. I had flashes of my sister dying, but I knew that was not the case this time around.

I was forced to sit down back in my chair when my head started pounding, I grabbed my laptop from my bed stand since I couldn't find my phone. The plan was to check my planner to see if I had written down what I could be trying to forget. I connected my laptop back to the Wi-Fi at home while I browsed through my reminders and planners. I realized the last time I had written anything in it was two weeks ago and I began to wonder if I had been in the hospital for two weeks. I saw so many future plans with Cindy and I wondered why I had not seen her yet. I noticed that we had planned to go on a trip together. I just couldn't remember what type of trip that was or if I had really gone on it. The day of the trip was also the last time I had updated my planner and so I knew that whatever must have happened to me must have happened after the trip. However, since I didn't have my phone, I knew there was nobody I could call and ask. I finally remembered that I could always send a message to my friends on their various social media platforms.

The first person's page I had opened was Kevin's and my body started going into another wave of shock again when I saw a lot of grieving messages on his feed. I wondered if something terrible had happened to Christy as I knew she was one person Kevin genuinely cared about no matter how much they loved to argue. What I saw next, however, shook the very core of my body; Kevin had posted about a candlelight service for Cindy. My brain became unable to wrap its head around why Cindy needed a candlelight service. The next post I saw was dedicated to Christy saying he was going to miss her, and no matter how hard I tried to understand what he was saying there was a part of my brain that did not want me to. The longer I stared at the computer screen the more the pain increased.

The memories came back to me like a leaking tap. I first saw Cindy's picture, which caused me to smile, and from then on I was able to allow my brain to think of her. I thought about the moments we had shared in my room and how happy she had made me feel. Then I remembered the carnival, and then the lake house. I remembered watching her lifeless body float on the water and I remembered Christy still struggling for help as her hands flapped in the water. I remember not being able to move as I remained frozen to the spot. I had known that Cindy was dead the moment I got to the lake. My mind had tried to prevent me from experiencing the same emotions I did when my sister drowned in our pool so it had completely shut down. I went towards my parents' room and knocked on their door like a crazy person.

"Is it true?" I asked my mother the moment she opened the door. I searched her face when she remained silent hoping for it to be a lie; however, she remained silent and I already deduced my answer from that. She held me tight expecting me to break down and cry, but I did not.

"I will be in my room," I said coldly. "Can I have my phone back?"

My mother looked at me in shock; she stared at me for a few seconds before rushing to get my phone.

"I will be here if you need me," she said in her very calm voice. "Please don't lock your door," she added, scared that I was going to harm myself.

I believe I never allowed myself to process the death of Cindy properly, in as much as I knew she was dead. I forced myself to pretend like I was fine; I phoned my friends and asked them to come over. They were shocked that I wanted them around and arrived a few minutes after I called them. When they came around, my mother told them I knew about Cindy's death and so they all walked towards me like I was an egg that could crack if they made any quick movement or said the wrong thing.

"How is Christy?" I asked the moment they had all found somewhere to sit in my room.

No one answered me for a few seconds as if afraid to

talk. I searched Kevin's face and found my answer there; he didn't look like he was in so much pain. At least not the kind of pain I knew I was trying not to feel.

"Her parents took her back to London from the hospital. I have not spoken to her yet, but I know she is getting better. At least that is what my mother says," Kevin said in a voice I had never heard him use before, he sounded like a struggling mouse that had been caught in a trap.

"I am glad she is fine," I said truthfully. I was glad she had survived. "Did she say what happened?" I asked, startling everyone a second time.

Tee looked at me like I had grown an extra head or I was being controlled. They were unable to believe I was really fine.

"Christy said they had gone for a swim, she said she had not been aware Cindy was not a good swimmer and they had chased each other around the lake. She said one minute Cindy was laughing at her and splashing water at her and the next minute she could no longer see Cindy. She said she had panicked as she had realized they had swum so close to the middle of the lake and had tried diving into the water to push Cindy back to the surface. She had also discovered she could no longer float again and that was when we saw her struggling in the water. Christy believed that the shock of knowing that they were in the middle of the lake must have been the reason she drowned. They had not been conscious of how deep the water was until that point and Cindy had drowned instantly from the fear," Paul said sadly.

I tried to remember what I had been doing while my girlfriend had been drowning in a lake; I had been watching a game and I was not there like I promised her. I knew if I was there she would not have died, I would have been able to carry her on my shoulders if I had discovered she could no longer swim. I blamed myself because I was unable to fulfill the promise I made to another person I loved. I stared into space while my friends remained silent as if expecting me to lash out at any second. They didn't realize that I was very confused at that moment and I could not act out since I was not sure of the way I was feeling.

"The candlelight service, when is it?" I asked Kevin this time around since I had gotten the information from his page.

"In two days," he said.

"Her uncle, did you see him?" I asked, trying to remember the last time I saw him. I wondered how much he hated and blamed me at that moment. He had expected me to take care of Cindy on our trip, but instead I ended up killing her. I knew there was no way I could face someone like that. I looked around the room at my friends' faces, they all looked like they were grieving. Cindy's death affected every one of us; she had come around and changed the dynamics of our little group without knowing it. I started remembering so many moments and I burst into laughter when I couldn't hold it in anymore.

"Do you remember when Cindy hid Kevin's toast in her bag?" I said to explain my sudden laughter.

Kevin smiled when he also remembered when that happened.

"He looked like a lost puppy," Becky added, smiling too.

"I assumed she was going to eat it; well, I wanted her to," Paul said as he smiled at Kevin.

"I can't believe she hid it so well, I wouldn't have known it was her if not for you guys looking at her and laughing," Kevin said.

We all remained silent for a few minutes before we started preparing for the candlelight service. Kevin had already taken control of most of the activities for the candlelight service, he had promised Christy he was going to honor Cindy's death and I realized he had done a good job so far. There was not much more to be done after we had finalized the arrangements for the candlelight service. Cindy was going to be buried the day after the service and I knew I didn't have the right to show my face there. My head started to bang and I knew I could no longer pretend I was fine anymore. "I would like to sleep," I said to everyone in the room.

"Are you sure you are okay?" Tee asked in a worried voice. I figured out they must have seen me rub my head and there was no point in lying to them.

"I have a headache," I said to no one in particular.

"Do you need us to call a doctor?" Kevin asked as he grabbed his phone.

"No, I believe I just need to sleep," I said as I made my way to my bed, not bothering to see them to the door.

"We will leave you to rest," Paul said and he asked the others to stand up so I could rest.

"Please do not hesitate to call me or any one of us," Kevin said, afraid I was going to shut him out again.

"I won't," I said as I closed my eyes.

When I was sure they had left, I was tempted to lock the door, but I knew how worried my mother would become if I did that. I climbed into my bed as the reality of what was happening started to dawn on me. I then began to laugh when I realized I could not let my mind believe that Cindy was really gone. I laughed for an hour and I almost ran out of breath because of how hard I laughed. Then I began to cry. At first, they were silent sobs until I couldn't control them anymore. I felt lifeless while I cried; I felt I was being punished for something because I knew life could not have been so unfair to me. I wondered what sort of life was worth living if everyone I loved just happened to die. My mother walked in on me crying and held me tight. Her embrace only made things worse; I cried more because I knew the cold hands of death could also snatch her from me. I wondered when that was going to happen. As I watched her cry with me, I wondered if she was also starting to notice that I was indeed cursed.

That night, I found it difficult to sleep just like on the day my sister died. I dreamt of Cindy that night; she was on a roller coaster ride while I was on the ground. I begged her to come down so I could join her, but she only smiled at me. She told me to stay down for her as she knew I was scared of roller coasters. She told me she was happy being up and promised to greet Star when she saw her. She begged me to be happy and wanted me to promise her. I refused because I knew I couldn't be happy without her. In this dream, Cindy kissed me one last time before going on her never-ending roller coaster ride. She didn't let me apologize to her before she left and that only made things worse. I felt I should have done so, it had been my fault that she had died and I had gotten to live while she had not. However, I hoped she met Star so she could look after her for me before I joined them.

I knew I wanted to join them both badly; I knew I had to apologize to them and let them know life was not worth living without them. I began to think of ways to kill myself. I pretended everything was fine to my friends and parents so they would give me enough space to plan my death. It was not easy at first as they all felt I needed to be watched every hour.

I decided to kill myself on the day Cindy was to be buried; I found the best way to combine all the drugs I was taking to help kill me. I wrote my farewell letter all through the night and stayed awake waiting for morning to come.

CHAPTER TWENTY-SEVEN

O n the day of Cindy's burial, I dozed off for a few
minutes and when I woke up all my drugs had gone.
My mother had become a very good detective ever
since I had tried to commit suicide after my sister's death; she
knew I was going to try something stupid again. I was not able
to attend Cindy's burial but my friends did, and my mother
had invited a new therapist to the house. I was told I was
suffering from chronic depression and I needed to start taking
a new batch of medicine.

"How do you feel today?" the new therapist asked me.
She introduced herself as Flora and I found it very odd that
she should be named that.

"I don't know," I said, wondering what really happened
to my other therapist. My mother said she had gone on a
vacation and decided not to come back again. I did not believe
her as I knew she had promised to always talk to me whenever
I needed her help.

"Do you feel sad?" Flora asked again.

"Sad?" I was confused as to why I should feel sad.

"Yes, your girlfriend is being laid to rest as we speak.
Don't you feel sad about it?"

"No, I do not," I answered truthfully. I was glad I wasn't being forced to go to the funeral. I just wished they had allowed me to die.

"Do you feel the need to kill yourself?"

I had begun to wonder why she was asking me very obvious questions.

"Yes, I do," I said and she began to write in her diary. I wondered if she had already concluded I was a crazy person.

"When did you start feeling this way?" she asked.

"Ever since my sister died."

"Why did you want to kill yourself today?" she asked me again.

"Because I killed Cindy and Star. I do not deserve to live," I said coldly.

Flora wrote some things down in her book again and I was tempted to ask her if I could see what she was writing.

"Cindy and Star drowned. That has nothing to do with you, Ken. You should not blame yourself for their deaths. I doubt they would be happy knowing that you want to kill yourself."

"You don't know them," I said, snapping at her. "I am sorry," I said as I adjusted myself in the chair and avoided her gaze.

"It's fine. Please do not hold anything back," she said, smiling at me.

I burst into tears the moment I saw her smile at me. She pulled out a box of tissues from her bag and handed it to me.

"Don't hold back the tears," she said as she got up to sit close to me. I looked at her and began to cry some more, I had not realized how much I was hurting until then.

"I wish I was strong enough to attend the funeral, I wish I could be there for her now," I admitted as I continued to sob.

"I might not know who Cindy is, but she sounds like a very nice girl. Your friends are also amazing people as they decided to stream the funeral service live so you could watch it if you want to. Do you want to watch it?" she asked, removing Tee's tablet from her bag.

"Yes, I do," I said in between hiccups.

Flora switched on the tab and we waited patiently for the connection to be restored. I grew very anxious because I was not sure of what to expect. I felt more relaxed knowing I was not there though; it felt better watching the whole ceremony through Tee's tablet. Cindy's uncle was saying a few words about her the moment we tuned in, I could hear and feel the pain in his voice and he stopped every minute to take a deep breath. It was so obvious he loved Cindy and I felt myself shake as I remembered I was the cause of this misfortune.

"It was not your fault," Flora said to me as she held me tightly. "We do not have to continue watching it if you do not feel up to it." She put her hand on the power button to show she was being serious.

"It is fine," I said, stopping her from switching it off. I knew I had to be strong as I knew it was what Cindy would have wanted. It felt very weird talking about her in the past tense on that day. We went back to watching the ceremony and I tried my best not to cry when I saw my friends get up on the stage and talk about Cindy. They all genuinely loved her and it broke my heart to see that they were all in pain too. Flora was already sniffing as she pulled out tissues from the tissue box she had earlier handed to me.

I could not look at the casket throughout the ceremony. Looking at it felt like I was finally acknowledging that Cindy was dead. So I looked everywhere but at the casket; I appreciated the décor and I knew Cindy would have loved it too as they had used her favorite type of roses. There was also a huge projector in the church that showed slides of pictures of Cindy. I found myself smiling when I realized she was a happy child, her smile was so bright that it crushed me to know that the world would be denied seeing that beautiful smile. I was so proud of how I held it in throughout the ceremony; I was able to hold all my tears in, and in the process of congratulating myself, I heard a voice that said everyone should move outside as it was time for Cindy to be laid into the ground. My eyes were unable to leave the screen and I froze at that point.

It was also at this time that I looked at Cindy's casket. She was dressed in a yellow print dress with a lot of sunflowers scattered around her hair. Even in death Cindy still looked like the most beautiful girl in the world. I found it hard to tear my gaze away from her closed eyes. She looked like she was sleeping and I expected her to wake up at any moment and declare that she had been joking all along. I wanted that to happen badly as that would have made things better for all of us, I knew I would have kissed her and told her how much I still loved her even if she did that. I knew everyone in the room would be willing to do just that too, and so I stared at her coffin long and hard until it was wheeled away. I didn't stop hoping even when she was lowered into the ground, I had never wanted a miracle as much as I desired one on that day. I was still hopeful even when the priest started his short sermon about life and death. I would have won the longest stare competition with how much I stared at the coffin on that day. I was finally able to accept that Cindy was never coming back again when her uncle poured dirt on her casket. I wished he would stop because he wasn't so sure that Cindy was really dead. Thereafter, I cried so much that I was hardly aware of anything in the two days that followed. When I woke up, I knew my friends had come to visit because I saw cards signed by them.

The weeks that followed Cindy's burial were almost like those that followed my sister's funeral; it felt like déjà vu when I followed the same grief pattern I had adapted during Star's death. I took my therapy sessions more seriously this time because I didn't want my friends or mother to worry. I knew I was not fine as I felt myself slowly dying away inside. Howver, I pretended I was fine so I could get my solitude, my solitude had become very precious to me as it became the only time when I could fully wallow in my pain without being asked if I was fine every minute or looked upon with pity. I would play my music not so loud that my mother would get suspicious but loud enough for me to cry without being heard. Sometimes I would stay awake just because I could not face the nightmares that had begun to haunt me whenever I closed my eyes. I asked for sleeping pills and they gave them to my mother who only gave me the required dosage, which had no effect on me, but I pretended it did so my mother would not think about my problems. Flora had suggested that my mother should be in control of all my drugs until I got better; she had not been so sure I was going to keep my promise about not committing suicide. I did not blame her as I knew I would have taken more than the required number of sleeping tablets if they were in my care.

CHAPTER TWENTY-EIGHT

I didn't take a break from school like I had done when my sister had died; everyone was shocked to see me in school that morning and I became the trending topic in school for the day in no time. My parents were actually the most shocked because when they had opened my door I was dressed and ready to go to school. They initially came to let me know that I could stay at home and they were ready to talk to the vice principal for me. I did not feel the need to stay at home this time around because I felt my body had already adapted to the grief system. I stopped crying and tried my best to forget Cindy altogether. Physically, I looked like I was better and had moved on; but inside me it looked like I was trying to cover an open gash without treating it first.

My swimming coach in school was the first person to see me, I had been walking in the school hallway when he saw me and stopped me.

"Ken?" he asked in shock.

I nodded my head and he just stared at me.

"How are you doing?" the coach asked with pity in his eyes. I decided to ignore this pity by giving him a fake smile.

"I was just going to get your house address again and mail

this letter to you," he said as he dangled the white envelope in his hands. "However, since you are here, I might as well let you just have it," the coach said as he handed me the envelope and waited for me to read it.

I looked at the letter for a few seconds then looked back at Coach Jeff's eager face. I knew if I failed to open it at that point I would definitely hurt his feelings. I knew I was not interested in knowing what was in the letter, but I was trying to avoid hanging out in the hallway for too long. I opened the letter slowly when I realized I had no choice but to do so. My eyes scanned what was written there. *"You are one of the successful candidates who we have chosen to join the US Olympics team."* I stared at the paper for a few minutes and the coach was forced to ask if I was alright. Being in the US Olympics had always been my dream; Cindy had been the one who had advised me to write to the talent manager there and they had responded by sending someone to my school. On the day he came I had not known there was someone like that in the audience and I had just put in my best because that was what I was used to doing. Winning the state championship had also been an added advantage for me as they could see that I was actually as good as I said I was. The competition during that swimming game was very tough and only the best were eligible to participate in the competition.

I found it difficult to describe my emotions as I held my letter, I tried to be happy inside but it was impossible. This felt like news I was supposed to have shared with Cindy, but she was not here and I didn't know if I was allowed to be happy after her death.

"I am proud of you, Ken," Coach Jeff said as he took my silence for happiness.

I looked at him and managed a smile. I was still unable

to feel the excitement I had assumed I would feel when I got this letter.

"I plan on sending a copy to Coach Arnold; I hope that is going to be okay with you?" Coach Jeff asked.

"Yes, it is fine."

"Congratulations once again, boy. I am sure your friends and family will be excited to hear this good news. I will have to reschedule your practice hours as you will need to put in more time. You are no longer just a state champion; you are on your way to being the best your country has seen," Coach Jeff said as he patted my back before leaving.

I remained rooted to the ground as I thought about what he had said, the gravity of the news was just finally dawning on me, and I knew I didn't feel like I was in the right place to accept such an opportunity. My mind went back to the last time I had actually considered representing the United States in their swimming competition. Cindy and I were walking hand in hand at the park as we discussed our future plans. She had blushed when I had teased her about her dream of traveling around Europe. She had wanted to be so many things that it was hard for me not to dream big also. I had joked that she would end up being the wife of a very hot swimming Olympics medalist. We planned to crash a party whenever I got the acceptance letter and eat all we could eat. She had even promised to get me a cake with my face on it and a lot of candles so it would take me all day to blow it out.

"I told Becky it was you I saw," Tee shouted from a distance as he walked towards me.

"Hi, Tee," I said, stuffing the letter into my backpack while throwing him a smile.

"We were all planning to come to the bakery when school was over."

"The bakery?" I asked, confused.

"Your mother said that you were going to be there if you didn't come to school."

I remained silent as I realized my parents did not trust me to stay at home alone. I could not blame them as I had given them no reason to feel otherwise.

"How was your weekend?" I asked, trying to change the topic.

"It was alright, my parents are back. Turns out I will be moving to Japan once senior year is over. My parents want me to go to a tech school there and oversee their company in Japan," Tee announced sadly.

"Wow, Japan is far away," I said, stating the obvious.

"I know, right?" Tee said dejectedly.

"What about golf?" I asked.

"According to them, they plan on building me a golf school where I can train kids to play golf. That feels like a better offer to me than giving up golf altogether."

"Well, you are right. So you have just a couple of weeks left in this school," I said as I looked around the hallway.

"Yes, it's unbelievable. Time really does fly."

"What are you guys talking about?" Kevin and Becky said simultaneously as they walked to where Tee and I were standing.

"Jinx," Kevin said, sticking his tongue out.

"Tee is moving to Japan," I said to neither of them in particular.

"Japan? But you do not even speak Japanese," Kevin said, alarmed.

"You have no British accent for someone moving back to England and you equally hate tea," Tee countered.

"Oh please, like those things can be compared to

not knowing how to speak a language in a foreign country. Just imagine if you had listened to me and you had started watching animes; I am sure we wouldn't be having this type of conversation right now," Kevin said.

I watched the two of them as they continued with their back and forth banter. I tried to fight a smile as I realized how much I would miss every one of them once they all left. Becky was also moving to London as he had gotten an offer to play for Liverpool. His parents were very hesitant about the offer, but they had eventually come around when Becky promised to video call his mother every day. Paul had still not been sure if he wanted to leave the United States yet and had decided to weigh his options before coming to any decision. I was not sure whether to tell them about my acceptance into the US swimming team. I felt I was happier knowing that they were all doing great for themselves. I wasn't sure if I deserved to feel happy at the present moment and so I ensured I focused on every word my friends had to say. It was a wonderful distraction for me and I was happy I had come to school.

When school closed, my parents asked me to come to the bakery as they had something they wanted to discuss with me. I feared the worst as I assumed they were going to tell me about someone dying. Kevin drove me there when he realized how pale I looked; he assured me several times during the ride that he was sure no one was dead. I was almost rude to him when he continued to act like he was so sure no one was dead. I walked slowly to my mother's bakery and was greeted by a lot of her staff members who wanted to offer their condolences. I was already shocked by the thousands of condolences I had received while in school from both my peers and the teachers. The vice principal had wanted me to give a speech after a one-minute silence was held for Cindy. I was glad I had declined the offer politely since I knew I wouldn't have been willing to give any speech concerning a girl my heart was still bleeding for.

"How was school today?" my mother asked as she came around to where I was standing to give me one of her warm hugs that always had the power to improve my mood. I walked into her office absentmindedly and so was unaware of the presence of my father and Coach Arnold in the room.

"School was fine," I said as I untangled myself from my mother's embrace and faced my father.

"Good afternoon, Father; good afternoon, Coach," I said as I bent my head slightly in acknowledgment of their presence.

"Take a seat," Coach Arnold said as he gestured towards one of my mother's chairs.

I sat down with wobbly legs as I feared the news that was going to be given to me.

"Do you want me to talk or would you like to do so?" Coach Arnold said as he turned to face my father.

"Sure, please go ahead," my father said, smiling. Seeing him smile was another reassurance I didn't know I needed to be sure that nothing was amiss like I feared.

"So we heard about your acceptance letter," Coach Arnold said as his straight face finally broke into a smile.

I didn't know I had been holding my breath in and I exhaled so loudly that everyone in the room turned to stare at me.

"Are you okay?" my mother asked as she ran to my side to start examining me.

"Yes, I am fine, I was just scared something was wrong when you called me in," I said truthfully.

"Oh, we are sorry if you made you feel that way," Coach

Arnold said as he came around to my side and gently squeezed my hand.

"I am okay now," I said, smiling.

My mother returned to her chair, while Coach Arnold continued to address me.

"How do you feel about joining the US swimming team?"

"Indifferent for now, I don't know if I would be able to measure up," I said to the coach. I didn't want them to think that I was not excited at the prospect of joining the swimming team because I knew my mother would never allow me to join if she knew I was not excited.

"You are an amazing swimmer, Ken. I have coached so many and I do not think anyone deserves this opportunity as much as you do. This is something you have earned because of how good you are. There is no way they would want you on their team if they did not realize how amazing you are. You can do this and Coach Jeff and I would be happy to guide you through every step of the way."

"The coach is right, Ken; you are the best swimmer in the world. Your love for swimming has taught us how necessary passion is in everything you do. Ever since you were a young boy, the water has always been your friend. Do not let a little fear limit you and cause you to doubt yourself. If there is anyone that I know who will bring glory to our country it is you. So please consider this as everyone in this room is ready to support and guide you every step of the way."

I remained silent as I considered everything they said, although I didn't agree with them calling me the best swimmer. I knew I couldn't let them know I didn't think the water was my friend anymore. It took two people dear to my heart and the idea of swimming while the whole country watched you sounded terrifying to me. I remembered how pressured I had felt during the state championship and I wondered if something worse was not bound to occur if I decided to join the US swimming team.

I looked around at the eager faces of the people in the room; I knew that as much as they wanted me to decide by myself, they all still wanted me to say yes. I knew it was a golden opportunity and rejecting the offer might come back to haunt me later.

"Yes, I will do it," I said as I looked at my parents and then my coach.

My mother immediately brought out a celebratory cake with my face as a cake stand. I laughed for the first time since Cindy died.

"I told you he would like the cake," my mother said as she placed it in front of me.

"Thank you," I said as I picked up the fork that was presented to me and took a forkful of cake.

"Do you want some?" my mother asked Coach Arnold. Coach Arnold was never a fan of anything made with sugar or from sugar; his response on this day, however, shocked me.

"Yes please," he said.

I looked at him in shock as he took his piece of cake and threw it into his mouth before sending a wink my way.

"Today is worth celebrating," he said before going to speak to my father privately.

"How did your friends take it when you told them?" my mother asked, still sounding very excited.

"I have not told them yet," I said to her.

"Why?" she asked, sounding worried all of a sudden. Sometimes I wondered how she was always able to switch from one emotion to the other so quickly.

"Today just wasn't a good time. I will tell them tomorrow," I said to reassure her.

I stayed back at the bakery with my parents that afternoon and ended up falling asleep without even knowing it. I dreamt of Cindy when I slept; I got to share my good news with her and she was very happy for me. It was one of those dreams I was very unwilling to wake up from.

CHAPTER THIRTY

The last few weeks of my high school life were spent training rigorously for the Olympics, I was told I was going to have a trial once I resumed at the SCOO. SCOO was an acronym for Swimming College of Olympians. My practice hours had become so time-consuming that I hardly had time for anything again. I rarely ate lunch with my friends as I was placed on a strict diet that was monitored by Coach Jeff. Everything felt like it was happening so fast and sometimes I felt like I was watching my body act of its own accord. I still felt depressed as I began to hallucinate about my sister and Cindy.

There were days when I would be in the pool and would hear my little sister call out to me. I would swim towards the voice and find out there was nothing there. I had saved enough money from working in my parents' store to buy some drugs that could help me. I had found out about them from a guy in my school whose dad was a pharmacist. The drugs helped for a while and soon I became addicted to taking them before I entered the pool. Coach Arnold noticed my odd behavior. So, one day, as I ran from the water, he sat me down to ask if I was really okay and I lied.

I was made valedictorian for my high school graduation and it took me weeks to come up with the perfect speech with the help of my friends. My friends all volunteered to help me out when they discovered I was stuck. We all agreed to meet at our favorite spot, which was Tee's house. Lance came over too. I had not seen him for a couple of months now as his parents made him go for various swimming competitions. Sometimes, I wondered if things would have been different if he had come on the trip with us. He was an excellent swimmer and I knew if there was anyone who could have saved Cindy, it would have been him.

"Lance, welcome!" Kevin said as he handed Lance a customized hat he had made for everyone in our group. He called it his parting gift. Kevin was returning to England immediately after our graduation, he had been able to convince Paul to join him and so he was finally excited about his trip back home. We also knew he had missed Christy and wanted to see her badly too.

"I heard about the good news," Lance said to me with a smile. "My parents almost flipped out when they heard you made the team, their regret now is not allowing me to be your friend earlier," he said, laughing.

I felt like Lance deserved to join the team instead of me, he had been training all his life to be a professional swimmer and I was sure he had never run away from the water like me. However, I never mentioned that out loud and kept my thoughts to myself.

"You would not believe how good my Japanese has gotten," Tee said once they had helped me with my speech.

"This guy here is a crook," Becky said, laughing.

"You just broke my heart," Tee said as he pretended to be hurt.

"He has been cheating in all his lessons and saw one season of *Naruto* before claiming to be an amazing Japanese speaker. He already claimed he wants to hire a translator who will follow him about when he gets there," Kevin said as he ate fries from his pocket.

"I doubt your parents would let you hire one," Paul said.

"They will, as long as I promise to learn the language," Tee said in a tired voice. "Language learning is not my strong suit," he admitted.

"I could be your translator," I suggested.

"What then happens to the dream of our country winning Gold next year?" Lance asked teasingly.

"I am sure they can win without me," I said truthfully. My friends, however, thought I was joking and began to laugh. I only wished they knew I was serious.

"It is so weird how we will all be scattered around the world. The reality of everyone going their separate ways in a few days feels realer than ever and I do not want it to happen," Kevin said sadly.

That night, we all had one last sleepover at Tee's place. I tried to enjoy everyone's company without thinking about my own problems and what my future might hold for me.

Graduation day came early and it was very emotional for all of us. Christy came around and we all felt like one big family one last time. I, however, knew my graduation would have been better if Cindy was around. I looked around the crowd and felt silly when I discovered there was nothing that could bring Cindy back. My parents and Coach Arnold arrived in the middle of the ceremony and my mother blamed their tardiness on my father who had been trying to look for the perfect suit to wear. When it was time for my speech, my friends cheered for me the loudest and every fear I had evaporated. I looked at them and then my parents the moment I mounted the podium.

"It is such a wonderful privilege to have walked the same hallway with you all. You guys have been unique in your way and I know the world is not ready to receive your awesomeness. I would like to thank my group of friends who have stood by me during the saddest parts of my life. I would like to thank my family and my two wonderful coaches, whose strength and advice have helped me persevere. I hope that the future smiles on everyone and I hope we all try to keep in touch with each other. The friends and connections we have all made in this school should never be taken for granted and I hope we all can use them wisely. When we all leave here today, I hope we can all look back on this day and smile. Congratulations to the class of fifty!" I said as a wave of deafening applause accompanied me to my seat.

There were so many pictures taken on that day that I promised myself to avoid the camera for some days. I battled with two conflicting emotions on that day; I wanted to be happy but I discovered I was not happy. I still felt like I did not deserve to be happy and I battled with this feeling all through the day while pretending to be happy amid my well-wishers.

I accompanied Kevin, Christy, Paul, and Mr. Greg to the airport. Mr. Greg, who was now very old, could not control his tears when we got to the airport. I feared he was going to collapse with the heavy sobbing he did. Kevin equally failed to hide his tears and we all hugged each other while crying. It was a memory I could never forget. It felt like we were all aware of the finality of the situation; like we all knew there was a likelihood of us not seeing one another again.

Tee and Becky left the next day and their absence began to tell on me the following week. I had not realized how much their presence had helped me. I began to feel like I had taken them for granted, especially when Lance left. Lance got a scholarship to a very wonderful university in Germany and was happy to leave the United States and pursue his career without the influence of his parents.

CHAPTER THIRTY-ONE

I booked my ticket for my flight a week before I was set to leave for Texas. I was told I had to participate in the preliminaries first before I could qualify to compete alongside my team members in the Olympics, which were taking place in France. I promised myself not to let the memory of the great time I had in France with Star hinder me from doing well. Coach Jeff, Coach Arnold, and my parents had all promised to come and watch me swim in Texas. I had been looking forward to leaving town as the absence of my friends only reminded me of the sad memories that the town gave me. I still had nightmares at night and sometimes I felt like I was losing my mind. I had decided to stop taking my medications because of the competition, I didn't want to jeopardize my only chance at making the team win as Coach Arnold and Coach Jeff would have been disappointed if I did so.

I took one last walk around the park before leaving for Texas. I had also found the courage to visit where Cindy was buried. This was something I had never done before and was so scared to do. I remember breaking down as I saw her tombstone. I knelt and placed her favorite flowers there. I apologized to her for not visiting her and cried terribly when I told her all that had been happening in my life. I told her how stuck I felt and how much I needed her and cried some more when I got no response from her. I did not leave her grave until it was 5:00 p.m. and when the attendant begged me to leave. Leaving there was one of the hardest things for me to do. I had wished that I could hold her one last time. I wished that I could hear her voice one last time. As I finally found the courage to leave, I knew I was not going to be back in a while and so I told her the jokes that she had always thought were funny. As I said the jokes out loud, I could hear Cindy's voice in my head as she laughed. It was a very precious moment for me. I went home that night feeling relieved. I met my parents at the door who had gotten worried because I had not picked up their calls. We all dined together as a family that night.

It was the day I left for Texas that Mr. Greg died, I did not know about this until after my race. My parents had not wanted me to go into shock. Even when I heard it, I took it just as hard. It killed me that I was not there for Kevin and I tried to make it up, even though the call charges between the two countries we were in were terrible.

When I got to Texas, I met my new coach, Coach Mane, and met a few guys who were part of the team. Unlike my other coaches, Coach Mane was not very welcoming, and I was quite surprised at his methods. He made me display some of my skills before the day of the main event and it was hard to know if he was impressed or not. When I told Coach Arnold about him, he told me that it was best to ignore someone like him. This was a piece of advice I wish I had taken to heart. I also received so much advice from Coach Jeff and he asked me a lot of questions related to my physical and mental state before I went to bed that night.

The next morning, I woke up earlier than my alarm clock; I was unable to find real sleep as I was very nervous. As I stepped up to the block for my race that would determine if I was still going to France or not, my stomach turned over like a motor. I knew I was in major trouble when I saw that I was in lane eight. The way races were structured made it difficult for someone from the exterior lanes to surge into the lead. You would often come in with a slower time, and you would have to deal with wake from the swimmers on the inside lanes, which pours over you with each stroke. And nothing created more waves than the butterfly stroke. As I shook my legs and my arms in preparation for the competition, I noticed that my family was somewhere in the upper deck, and so were Coach Arnold and Coach Jeff. In the sea of spectators, I picked them out easily. I could see Coach Arnold mouth something to me, which I could not understand, and I decided to just pay attention to the competition at hand.

"Take your mark."

I bent and curled my fingertips around the edge of the block. I tensed my muscles, imagining them compressing like springs. Less than a second after the signal sounded, I hit the surface with the force of a torpedo. Water coursed over my shoulders and back, and I forced my head down, keeping a near-perfect streamline position as I kicked to the fifteen-meter mark before powering into my first stroke. The sound of Coach Arnold's voice echoed in my head: *You're a champion, so swim like a champion.* I decided to chant this in my mind as I kicked the water effortlessly. I ensured that I started with a technique I was good at, which was the butterfly. The butterfly works in a way where the arms come out to the side like wings as the head dips and the body undulates like a wave. Then the arms enter the water together, and your hands make a keyhole shape, pushing forward with another kick and gaining momentum for the next stroke. It was a very beautiful swimming skill I would always prefer.

Coach Arnold had taught me to breathe every few strokes, and thanks to Coach Jeff's hypoxic sets it was easier to fight the urge to lift my head up. I turned my brain off and let my body lead me through the butterfly, I did not strain or panic when it felt like I was not going fast enough. My goggles were fogging, so I was unable to see my competition at some point.

It was just me and the water, and it felt like the truest love story I have ever known. I felt like I was finally one with the water. As I changed into the backstroke, Coach Arnold's advice came back to me in pieces, soft and flimsy like tissue paper. I have always liked the backstroke because you never have to stop breathing. But in lane eight, with the wake of the other swimmers crashing over the lane line and ricocheting off the gutter, controlling my breath was the only way to prevent water from going up my nose. I concentrated on my technique, remembering everything Coach Arnold and Coach Jeff taught me, getting the most out of my arms and centering myself in the lane. The backstroke was over before I realized it, and I was into the next fifty. The breaststroke feels like the natural way to move through the water, but it is slow, so swimming that way during competition takes a lot of concentration and endurance. Of all the strokes, it requires the most technical precision. If your form is off, you can end up practically swimming in place.

I had to focus because I could see myself already getting distracted. I noticed that when I got to this point in a race, I sometimes began to founder, like a ship that could not be righted. I bulldozed through the breaststroke in a way that felt like flying; then I turned into the freestyle leg and let myself go. I had managed to conserve some energy and I decided to sprint hard. I charged through the first twenty-five and knew that I had clocked one of the fastest splits in my career so far. With my goggles so fogged up, I couldn't see anything but the thick black line along the bottom of the pool. I swam harder in the last twenty-five meters of that IM than I had ever done in my life and slammed into the finish, punching the touchpad so there would be no doubt about when I hit the wall.

I stayed underwater, eyes closed, afraid to rise to the surface and look at the scoreboard. I knew that if I came in eighth, I would have killed myself. If my time was, however, higher than the Trials cut, I knew all my problems would be over. Panting, I stripped off my goggles and got out of the water. Before I could see the board, I saw my mother and Coach Jeff jumping up and down in the stands, and I knew immediately that I had done something good. I forced myself to look at the scoreboard. I had beaten my own record.

"Oh my God," I gasped, sinking back into the water. "I am going to join the Olympics team." The realization of this hit me like a bullet as I hugged my parents who had come down to meet me.

The following weeks to come shaped my entire future. I left for France shortly after qualifying for the team. Training in France was nothing like any of the training I had received back at home. We were always awoken at very odd times to begin our training. Coach Mane also made it his duty to be a pain in my butt. It turned out that he and Coach Arnold had been rivals and he had decided to punish me for having a coach he did not like. I made some new friends in France who were also part of the team, and they had reminded me so much of my friends from high school who I had rarely been keeping in touch with. Every one of us had become busy and the different time zones only made things worse for us.

CHAPTER THIRTY-TWO

"What do you mean you are not going?"

It was a Sunday, Tall Dave and Dwayne had been texting me all afternoon asking if I was going to the party at Gina's friend's house and they wanted to know if they could come with me and if I had thought about Coach's offer of waiting till next year before I decided to compete. It was a thought that had actually been flying through my head ever since Coach said it. I was still a newbie and even though I had an amazing record, competition in the Olympics was no child's play and I was not sure if I was ready for it yet. However, I knew I could not waste the efforts of my coaches back at home and not do anything. I knew they would prefer I lose than not participate at all. I kept putting them off about the party because I honestly could not make up my mind, but around 5:00 p.m. I decided; I was going to skip it. I had never been a big fan of parties and from what I heard it never ended well. I still felt I should be mourning and so having too much fun was not something I was actually looking forward to. The only reason why I had even welcomed the idea was that I knew parties served as a distraction and a distraction was something my mind had needed at that point.

Telling my new friends that I was not going to the party did not go over well with them. They had been the first friends I had made since I moved down there, and they had shown me around and had stuck by my side ever since. Tall Dave, who was an extremely tall person, was an excellent swimmer despite his height. Dwayne was also exceptional and they were both in the same swimming category. It was only when we swam that we often got separated because Coach always wanted everyone to know their place. It was a ridiculous philosophy to me as I felt everyone should be able to help each other to get better.

I was finishing up the last of the list of homework my coach had given me when my phone rang. It was Dwayne.

I put him on speaker.

"Did you hit your head?" he asked.

"I don't think so. Maybe I did and it erased my memory, like in a telenovela. Why?"

"Then what possible reason do you have for not going to this girl's party?"

"She's too much pressure. She is too loud, and too nice, and too ... just too ... too ... everything, okay?"

"Wow, that's a lot of toos. You are spiraling."

I sighed. "Yeah."

"Okay, so, counterpoint: you don't have to marry her. It's just a party. A little flirting, a little kissing, maybe, then you go home and enjoy the fact that a girl who likes you invited you to her party and you can think about this for a couple of days. Plus, I bet she would be amazing in bed. The nice ones are always the wild ones. Have you never heard of that saying before?"

"What happens after a couple of days?" I ask, ignoring that last part of his conversation. Dwayne always had a take-no-prisoners approach to love. He often treated it the way he treated everything else: like a battlefield.

"You move on to another girl. At least, that is what I do," Dwayne said confidently.

"I know. The pool deck is littered with the shards of your exes' broken hearts," I said teasingly.

"Don't be melodramatic. They can't be exes because they were never girlfriends. They were crushes. There is no harm in a crush, but no girlfriends till next August."

For Dwayne, girls were a healthy distraction from the rigors of training, but only in a noncommittal sort of way. He had this superstition that being in a relationship would compromise his chances of making it to the Olympics.

As superstitions go, it was not that unreasonable, but that was the first time I gave it much thought. I had never been a casual dater and I was no casual anything. I had never liked any girl minus Cindy enough to consider something more serious. With all that had been happening to me, putting my career in jeopardy at that moment was something I did not want to start, especially since I had to constantly remind myself that I was still in mourning.

"Note that he didn't say anything about boyfriends," Tall Dave chimed in. "I can have as many boyfriends as I want. Not that I have any, but in theory."

"No boyfriends either," Dwayne said.

"Damn," Tall Dave said with mock disappointment. He was always telling me not to take what Dwayne said so seriously.

"Hey, Tall Dave, I didn't realize you guys were together. What are you doing?"

"Going on a mission," Tall Dave said in a low voice that I guessed was supposed to be mysterious.

"What kind of mission?" I asked because he was starting to sound suspicious.

"You'll find out very, very soon," Dwayne replied. Then he hung up.

A second later, my bedroom door flew open as Dwayne and Tall Dave stormed in.

Sam and Jerry, two dogs I had gotten when I had moved, were napping on my bed. They started and streaked out of the room. Fissle whistled from where he perched on top of his cage. He loved visitors. "Hola, bella!" he chirped.

Dwayne, who hated birds, shot Fissle a dirty look, but Tall Dave pointed to himself and said, "Fissle, say Tall Dave. T-all D-ave."

"Hola, Dave!" Fissle said then launched into a few bars of a song.

"You're hopeless," Tall Dave told Fissle with a disappointed eye roll.

"You didn't pick the lock on the front door, I hope," I said.

"Bells let us in," Dwayne said, gesturing over his shoulder. Nina was standing in the doorway with Sam cradled in his arms like a baby, smirking at me.

"Go to a party, Ken," he said. "It'll be good for you." Then he left.

I almost called after him to stay; we hardly ever saw each other, and I missed him sometimes. We used to have fun together. We were close once. We joined KAC together, a long time ago, but he wouldn't want to hang out with me and my friends, except maybe Christy, who he had always liked. He never spoke much once he grew up and the only time I ever remembered him calling was weeks after my sister died. He had called to let me know his parents had made him call me and he was very sorry about it. He had not talked about Star's death and had ended the call when I told him I did not mind his call. This was why when my parents had suggested he lived around my college and had a few rooms to spare, I was surprised he had agreed to me using his room or living around him. We had, however, gotten more accustomed to each other now.

"Listen to your distant cousin. He's older than you and therefore very wise,"

Tall Dave said, "You are going to this party, sir, and we are going to wait until you are ready even if it takes forever." I assumed they were joking and I put on a show on my computer. A few minutes into the show, I heard their laughter and I turned to look at them suspiciously. They had both complained at the beginning of the show that I was wasting their productive time by putting on a show that wasn't going to make any sense. I was tempted to.

"What'd you say this girl's name was?" Dwayne asked, backing into the street.

We had been driving for over four hours and I had started to wonder if we were not lost indeed. I could, however, see the map from where I was seated so I knew we were not entering into any lost forest.

"Telma?"

"Tela," I replied.

"I don't know any Tela, do you?"

Tall Dave and I shook our heads. The swim life is all-consuming. We pretty much didn't know anybody who was not on the team.

Tela's house was even smaller than mine, one of the squat three-bedroom ranch houses in the older part of town, but it was hard to miss with all the cars crammed in the driveway and lining the street. Dwayne double-parked in front of the house. The guy had, like, a hundred tickets; I didn't know how he still had his license. We made our way to the door. My palms were so sweaty that I had to wipe them off on my jacket. I thought my outfit looked good, thanks to Tall Dave, who stuck to his promise of not going overboard when he styled me. I looked like a happy person on the outside and on the inside I felt very broken as I wondered why people even wasted time coming to parties like this. I began to panic silently as I wondered if someone in my team would finally realize I was the swimmer who had lost both his sister and girlfriend in a pool. I wondered if they would respect me as much as they did now or if they would just kick me to the curb. I felt like I was betraying someone by coming to the party, I knew I wasn't going to have fun and I wondered why I was wasting my time there in the first place. I could feel my head pound from the loud music already and I tried not to let my discomfort show so my new friends would not find me weird.

Tela's house was even more cramped on the inside than it looked on the outside. The rooms were tiny; the hallway was narrow and dark; the oversized furniture was worn out. An enormous TV took most of one entire wall in the living room, and the floor in front of it was littered with gaming consoles and controllers. Hip-hop blared from a giant subwoofer near the window. Gina mentioned Tela's mom, but there was no sign that anyone but a teenage boy lived there. Even with a party going on, the place seemed kind of lonely. There was hardly any room to stand; people were stuffed in every corner of the place. Most of them had red soda cups in their hands, which I'm sure did not contain soda. I did not recognize anybody. The number of people in the room made my head start to spin and my first regret of the day was starting to show.

"Kitchen," Dwayne said, pulling me by the hand through the front room. The closet-size kitchen was at capacity, but Dwayne managed to thread us through the crowd. He bounced off to fetch us all something to drink, and Tall Dave started introducing himself to people he did not know, as was his way. My shoes stuck to the old-fashioned linoleum; someone must've spilled something. There was a black trash bag slumped at my feet, overflowing with cups and cans and I pitied whoever was going to clean up. This was another reason why I hated parties.

I scanned the room for Gina, but she was not there. I considered texting her, but I didn't want her to get the wrong message as all I wanted was for her to know that I was around.

"Dave, Dave, hey!"

I turned to see Gina slipping through a knot of people near the doorway.

When their eyes met, they lit up like a Fourth of July sparkle. They could not help it.

He was beaming that megawatt smile at her, and I could feel the electricity from them. I had never been around a guy and a girl with so many sexual vibes before. It was exciting and terrifying. I was scared they were going to start making out right there and then.

Gina looked great in a pair of dark jeans and a flowery T-shirt that seemed soft and showed off her swimmer's physique to maximum effect. If she was in my town, my mom would one hundred percent have said she should have been a boy, after which I would have died of embarrassment, but it was true. Her red-gold hair was shorter than it was yesterday like maybe she got it cut that afternoon, and the lighter strands glowed like the filaments in an antique light bulb.

As she approached where Dave stood, I admired the

color of her eyes, which Dave had said were the loveliest part of her; the blue of her shirt made them look like pools of indigo ink. Dave and Gina were always denying their love for each other and so I was made to act like the one Gina liked and hang around them even though they always wanted to have sex with each other at any given opportunity.

"You came!" she shouted over the music.

She moved closer to Tall Dave; Tall Dave went in for a bear hug, but it turned into one of those awkward one-armed sideways hugs. I wondered if he thought giving her a real hug would give people the wrong impression or was there just not enough room to use both arms? Maybe Dwayne and Tina were wrong about her liking him as more than a friend. It would make way more sense if she didn't. I wondered why Tall Dave's hand would not stop sweating as I saw him rub his hands on his jeans several times. Tall Dave was never nervous so it was fun seeing him like this.

"It's great to see you," she said.

"You saw me yesterday!" I told her.

Gina looked down at her shoes, a pair of battered old Nikes, but her smile didn't waver.

"Yeah, well, it's still nice. I wasn't sure you'd make it."

"Tall Dave and Dwayne brought me here," I confessed. I nearly said dragged, but I didn't want her to take it the wrong way.

She grinned. "What do I owe them?"

"A hundred and seventy-five dollars, before tax, and don't forget to tip your kidnapper," Dwayne said, appearing at my elbow with three drinks balanced precariously in his hands—a beer, a bottle of water, and a soda.

"Worth every penny," Gina said, taking the two cups. He handed me the beer and smiled at Tall Dave.

I shook my head. "I don't drink."

"Me neither," she said, switching my beer out for the soda.

"Suit yourselves. I'm DD, so none for me either." Dwayne cracked open his water.

"I'll just hold this for Tall Dave," Gina said. I smiled at her.

"I'm here, I'm here," Tall Dave said, emerging as if by magic out of a clump of strangers. He took the beer from Gina. "Thank you, my lady. That was very gallant of you."

"That's me," Gina said, bowing at the waist and flourishing her hand theatrically. "Gallant."

Tall Dave tapped his forehead. "It's never too early to start studying for those SATs."

"Gallant is not an SAT word," Dwayne said with a sniff. He was very intense about standardized testing. His parents had started enrolling him in prep classes back in eighth grade.

"You look really nice," Gina told me. Dave had chest cramps, and I realized he was holding his breath. "But then you always do."

"Right answer," Tall Dave said, punching her arm in a friendly way. He winced and shook out his fist. "What are you made of, lady? Rocks?"

"Petrified Red Vines, mostly," I said. Gina laughed and patted her back pocket; there was a half-empty pack of licorice sticking out of it.

My friends looked at each other like they were about to say something we would all regret.

"We should—" Tall Dave began, but he was cut off mid-sentence by the arrival of a white boy I did not recognize. He flung his arm around Gina's shoulders and sort of jostled her.

"Hey, girl, I lost you," the boy said.

"Well, now you've found me," Gina replied with a good-natured roll of her eyes. The boy seemed a bit buzzed. Gina shot him a wary look like she was afraid her friend might say something to embarrass her. "Guys, this is Tela. He goes to our college too. This is his house, his party. Say hi, Tee."

"Hi," Tela said. Gina introduced us, but Tela barely feigned interest.

He came over here for a reason, and he focused on that.

"Gina, the people are demanding a show," Tela told her, punching her arm repeatedly. Okay, maybe he was more than buzzed. Tela was a skinny guy with a medium build, so I doubt it hurt, but Gina pulled away and held up a hand to fend him off.

"Not tonight, man," she said. She gave Tall Dave an apologetic smile and I could tell he was already breathing heavily beside us.

Tela grabbed Gina by both shoulders. "But the people, Gina. Think of the people."

Gina laughed. I could tell she was uncomfortable, maybe a little nervous. I could tell Tall Dave wanted to pull her into a quiet corner, away from everyone, which is probably what a person with no anger issues would have done, but he just stood there with a murderous glare in his eyes.

"What are they even talking about?" I wondered aloud.

"The people are going to have to learn to deal with disappointment," she said.

"Really? I thought you'd do it just to impress this one." Tela angled his head at Tall Dave.

Tall Dave narrowed his eyes at him as his face grew hot. Between the temperature and the embarrassment, he was red as a stop sign at that moment.

Gina glared at Tela. Something about the way they

interacted reminded me of my distant cousin. Tela got under Gina's skin in the way only siblings or longtime friends did. "More like horrifying. I'm not doing it."

"Doing what?" Tall Dave asked.

"You'll see," Tela said with a wink.

"No, he won't," Gina shot back, giving Tela a light shove. To Tall Dave she said, "It's stupid."

"I want to see it now, whatever it is," Dwayne said, crossing his fingers. "Please be a strip show."

"Me too, me too!" Someone we had not known was standing beside us agreed. "Although I'm cool if you keep your clothes on."

Tela turned to Tall Dave. "What about you, Tall Dave? Don't you want to see the Flow?"

"It's Dave to you," Tall Dave said. I could tell he did not like Tela. "And I don't know what the Flow is."

"Believe me, it's great," Tela said, ignoring Gina's angry stare.

"Okay, sure. Let's see it," I said, giving Gina an encouraging smile. Tela's wasn't giving up. Maybe if Gina did what he wanted, he would leave us alone.

"Fine," she said with a world-weary sigh. "Let's go prep the stage."

"The stage? What is happening right now?" I muttered as they walked away.

Tela threw his arm around Gina's shoulders again, but Gina shook him off gently.

Tall Dave looked bothered, but Dwayne was so preoccupied with a text he just got that I didn't think he heard me.

"You. Guys." He looked up from iPhone, wide-eyed. "Remember Kara Walker?"

"Sure," Tall Dave said.

"What about him?" I asked.

Kara was a few years older than us, one of the best swimmers ever coached at that college. He swam for Boston and the previous year at the NCAA Championships he placed first in all of his events except one. I'd always looked up to him.

"He has got a girl pregnant. Apparently, it's a boy. Mazel tov, I guess," Dwayne murmured. He returned the text so fast I was surprised he didn't hurt his fingertips. "Lucy says Karal met a girl at Stanford and they started going out and now, buh-buh-boom—bun in the oven."

"How?" I sputtered.

"Don't make me explain where babies come from. My version does not involve storks."

"I mean he's supposed to go to the Olympics. Everyone had him pegged for a multi-gold contender! He can't train if he has a pregnant wife, and he can't go to the Olympics if he doesn't train."

"He could leave his girlfriend and deny the baby—Dara Torres did," Tall Dave said.

"Not everybody is Dara Torres," Dwayne argued. "His life is going to majorly change. It could throw everything off. He might never get back to where he was competitively."

The mention of starting a career struck a nerve. Of the three of us, I knew best how that could affect your entire career, maybe even end it. I wanted to keep talking about this, I couldn't wrap my mind around the fact that Karal Walker wouldn't be going to the Olympics—but the squeal of a microphone distracted me.

On the other end of the room, Tela was standing in front of the kitchen island, which was now entirely cleared of chip bowls and abandoned drinks and other party debris. He was holding a portable karaoke machine in one hand and a wireless mike in the other. Everyone became quiet. Tela cleared his throat.

"Ladies and gentlemen," he said, his voice reverberating through the tiny speaker. "I give you ... the Flow."

A familiar hip-hop song started playing on the stereo and Gina took a flying leap off a chair positioned in the corner, landing in a crouch on the island. Her momentum carried her a bit too far and one of her feet slipped, but she righted himself. I suspected she had practiced this. Tela tossed the mike at her and Gina snatched it in midair. Then she stood up, closed her eyes, and started to rap. The room erupted in applause and cheers. Most of them seemed to have been expecting this.

"This is her party trick," Tela said, wedging himself in beside me. "People love it."

That was clearly true, but the best part was that despite how reluctant she seemed earlier, Gina loved it too. It was obvious how happy it made her get the lyrics right, how good she felt slicing the air with her hands in time to the beat. She was holding the mike like a beloved thing, rolling her shoulders and swaying her hips, and dropping rhymes. She looked ridiculous.

Except, because she didn't seem to care what she looked like, or what anybody thought, she careened right past the threshold of ridiculous and looped back to awesome. I felt weightless like the floor had suddenly vanished from under my feet. All these people were way too cool for me. I didn't know why I thought, for even a second, that I could be friends with them or that, with my career in such a fragile state, I had any business trying to make friends.

I looked for a way out of the crowded room and ran out of the house. I ran in no particular direction as I knew all I wanted to do was be free again. I wondered if my life would ever go back to the way it was before, the days when I had been very happy and free. It seemed like it had been ages since I had smiled. It also looked like I might never get to smile again. Coming to the party had been a mistake and as I stood panting, I realized I couldn't have friends. I was already too broken and I was tired of making friends. I just felt like I was deceiving them by being someone I was not. For now, swimming seemed like the only thing that made any sense to me and I decided to concentrate on that. I knew I could look back when I won and smile at the decision I was making at that point.

CHAPTER THIRTY-THREE

On the day of the race, I was in the room where we got ready as I tried to calm my nerves. Everything felt like déjà vu. I was wearing the same swimming gear that I had worn during the state championship, the same music I had listened to on that day was blaring through my headphones, and there were many familiar faces around, waiting for their race to begin. However, the air in the environment was thick with new tension and nervous energy that was hard to define. I felt as if I could see everyone's thoughts spiraling through the air like threads cast from a spool; their mantras and doubts, fears, and hopes. I wondered if they could see mine. None of us knew what was going to happen out there. So many races had been lost and won in that pool already. Shoe-ins had triumphed and slunk home in defeat; rising talents had toppled icons and faded into obscurity. I had always believed that nothing could be compared to the moment a race started. It was the highest height of the roller coaster, the top of the drop, all potential energy and anticipation. That powerful feeling of launching off the block was my favorite thing about swimming, the weightlessness of flight before slipping neatly into the water.

Despite all the disappointments of the past few years, the excitement before the start never left me, and this day was no exception. The simple act of climbing onto the block flooded my body with adrenaline. A calmness like none I had ever known before settled over me like a light blanket. There was a peculiar feeling in my shoulders, not pain, but rather a slight, comforting weight, as though fate had settled its hands on me. It felt like a benediction, a sign of what I had suspected since the first trial: that my destiny had finally caught up with me. Now that we were together again, my dream was ripe for the plucking.

My vision narrowed, and all the noises of the pool—the slap of waves against the gutters, the shouting from the stands, the voice of the announcer as he called out the names and positions of the swimmers already in the water—receded like a tide until I heard nothing but the sound of my own breathing.

However, the real surprises hadn't happened yet. Everyone on my team had been aiming for one of the two Olympic medals, but I knew I did not just want to win. I wanted to take their breath away. I was at the Olympics.

The air was alive with thousands of voices murmuring speculatively in the vast cathedral of the natatorium, but in my head everything was quiet. I looked around and mapped these last seconds of possibility with clear eyes: the lights and the cameras, the coaches and the crowd. Judges took their places at either end of each lane, on a sharp lookout for infractions. The water rippled in slow motion beneath me, calling to me in a language only we shared. *Come and find yourself here,* I imagined it saying.

'Take your mark,' the announcer commanded over the loudspeaker.

A sudden hush cascaded through the arena.

All the terrible thoughts dissolved the very moment the water touched my skin. Many times, in the past two years, no matter the result at the end, my body always felt heavy and cumbersome in the water. However, today was different as I felt like a feather coasting on a current of air, a particle of light shooting through the vacuum of space. My arms sailed forward like wings then pulled back again as they pushed me forward with the strong and steady rhythm of the butterfly. The ease of it was exquisite, the lack of strain or struggle, but I hardly had time to marvel at how good it felt before the first fifty meters were over and I went into the backstroke. Everything went so fast. I could not manage complete thoughts as the water churned around me with the fury of a sea in a storm, obscuring my vision so thoroughly that I missed the flags at the fifteen. Instinct took over, and I flipped just in time to get a strong push off the wall.

The first race started with the 200 m backstroke, and the breaststroke came next. The third leg of this race, the butterfly stroke, belonged to me. Derek was behind me, hands on his hips, dripping wet and he was still panting. He had started strong, touching the wall first with one of his best backstroke splits. Brian, our anchor, stood to the side, watching and waiting for his turn. In the pool, Charles held on to Derek's lead with his high-velocity whip kick and came at me with full speed. My skin started to tingle, not from anticipation but from a sudden sizzling lightning bolt of fear, the fear of screwing up that blossomed inside me like an infinitely expanding fractal. That fear was an old enemy and yet sometimes startlingly new. Even at that moment, when I should have known what to expect, it snuck up behind me and leaped on me, causing the air from my lungs to cease and wrapping its arms around my chest so tightly that I could hardly breathe. But there was nothing I could do about it; I was already on the block. As Derek closed in on the wall, I made the calculation; that inexplicable formula learned through what seemed like a million years of racing. I gave it one Mississippi, two Mississippi, three, and then I jumped again. The moment I hit the water, my instincts told me something was off, but everything felt okay. I was an arrow beneath the surface; the momentum from my dive, my painstakingly perfected streamline, and my powerful dolphin kick was enough to get me to the fifteen-meter mark before my head broke the waterline. Arms back, then out, and then I was flying. My muscles were tense, and the first few strokes were a struggle while I searched for my rhythm. Once I found it, my body melted into the swim so naturally that it came more as a surprise than a relief.

I had not felt this good, this capable, for months. Even my left arm, which sometimes bugged me, was not a problem on that day. Fear loosened its grip, and a rush of water carried it away. By the first turn, I began to feel cautiously optimistic, and by the second, I was almost hopeful, though I could tell from quick spot checks that my creakiness at the start had lost me some of Derek and Charles's lead. I knew I could make it up. I had done it before, and I knew I could do it again. Otherwise, all of my training would have been for nothing. The surge of confidence pushed me harder into each stroke, and by the final lap, I had caught up with the swimmer on my left, who passed me at the midpoint of the race.

I immediately felt a shift as I switched into the breaststroke. Never my favorite, breaststroke is a point where you shine only if you are going by technicalities. My form was good, my execution nearly perfect, but there was something bloodless about the way I swam the breaststroke that I had never been able to change. Even then, in the most crucial moment of my life, the spark that animated me through the backstroke and the butterfly gutters died. The lightness I felt in the first two laps was gone; my limbs felt thick and rubbery. I tried not to panic, but I felt myself thrashing, and in the breaststroke that could sink you. It suddenly became as if I was not moving at all.

Water does not fight; water flows, I told myself as I clung desperately to the thought like a fallen climber scrambling for purchase on a rocky cliff. I tried to relax my limbs, to be like the water.

Arms like water, hips like water, legs like water, breath like water, I continued. A wail rose inside of me, pressing against my ribs until I had to let it out. I screamed into the water, lunging for every last foot as all the shitty things I had ever thought about myself cycled through my brain. *You cannot do this. You never could. You should give up.* I shoed those thoughts away, rejecting their premise. *I can do this, and I will not give up. I am too close; it is too possible, and I will gut this out to the finish.* I was about to hit the button when I saw Cindy's lifeless body in the pool. I made a costly mistake as fear gripped me, and I collapsed and hit the wall.

Over the PA, the announcer broadcasted the first-place finish. I was still so shaken by what had just happened that I remained frozen on the spot immediately I came out of the water. I could not bear to look at anyone in the eyes because I felt suddenly exposed, like in one of those dreams where you looked down to realize you were naked. But this was different; it felt like everyone knew something I did not know and they were all waiting to see the truth crash down on me. I could hear the disappointed murmurs from the crowd as I tried to swallow the tears that were threatening to fall. It was excruciating. Coach Mane pointed at one of the officials assigned to watch our lane for infractions as he scurried over to the judges' table. They huddled, whispered, and then broke apart. Coach Mane turned his finger to the ceiling, and, as if on cue, the announcer got back on the PA.

"Ladies and gentlemen, the judges have disqualified the US team for a reckless lane switch by Ken."

I stopped listening as a wave of hot shame poured over me. Charles, who stood next to me, put a gentle hand on my shoulder and squeezed it.

"Don't beat yourself up," he said. "It happens."

"Yeah, I know," I said with forced lightness. Sometimes I wished he was not so understanding because I knew I did not deserve his comfort or anybody else's. I failed them. I failed, yet again. My muscles shook from exertion, and I felt kind of faint. I needed to warm down, drink some water, and eat an energy bar. But I could not move; my gaze was locked on Coach Mane.

He had been looming over the judges' table, arguing against the DQ the way he would for anyone else; wild gestures, flying spittle, red-faced bluster, the whole coach being a sore loser kind of thing. But I could tell his heart was not in it. It had never been the judges he was angry with; it was me.

After the judges had calmly and firmly told him to get over it and go away, Coach Mane stalked over to me. I wrapped my goggles around my hand, tight enough to hurt, and stood my ground with my chin up and my mouth clamped shut. There was nothing Coach Mane could say to me that I had not been thinking about already. I believed that he could not make me feel worse than I already did.

"Disqualified!" he shouted, swinging his clipboard like

he was about to hit me with it, though he didn't. "At one of the biggest competitions, watched by millions of people around the world."

I took a deep breath.

"I know. I'm so sorry."

"What the hell was that?" he asked, loud enough for everyone around us to hear. Derek, Brain, and Charles had wisely made themselves scarce.

"It was an accident," I told him. "I made a mistake."

"A switch of lane at the end isn't a mistake. It is just thrash," Coach Mane hissed. "You are too old for this nonsense!"

My jaw clenched so tightly that my head started to ache. "I didn't do it on purpose. It won't happen again."

Coach Mane folded his arms across his chest. The tattoo on his bicep peeked out from under his sleeve—Olympic rings. His medals, two bronzes and silver, hung in frames on the wall of his office, not up to twenty feet from where we stood. Every time I was with him, I was forced to wonder why I put up with his sort of silly treatment. Still, I had always told myself, *He is an Olympian, and he makes Olympians. That is why he has been made to coach us.*

He scowled at me like I was a speck of dirt on his shoes. I had grown a lot during my few months of being in France, but I knew he thought I could never be as great as he was. No matter how old I was, I knew he would always look down on me.

"It will happen again," he snapped. "Or something else will. For the past few months, it has been one problem after another, except this time it's not just you. Your teammates are suffering because of what you did. That win was theirs, and you lost it."

"The win was ours," I reminded him. "And so was the loss. I swam that race too."

"You might as well not have. I could have put one of those plastic duck toys in the pool in your place and it probably would've had better splits!"

I was used to getting dressed down by Coach Mane. It had happened all the time. But the insult hit me so hard that I took a step back, feeling like he had smacked me.

"I had a good swim," I protested.

"You had an average swim," Coach Mane sneered, "which was worthless because it didn't count. Most of the time, you can't even manage that. You'd better figure out if you really want this, Ken, because it doesn't seem like it. And even if you do, I'm starting to wonder if you have what it takes. I don't think I can help you," he said before leaving me standing all alone.

I ran into the warm room and cried my eyes out inside the pool of water; I was glad no one knew I came to France because of my race. I could only imagine how disappointed they would be in me.

I got my first beer that night, I knew there was no way I could get a prescription on my own and so I turned to alcohol instead. I heard my phone ring a thousand times, but I refused to respond to it. I could already tell what they were about to say. I could see the pity in people's eyes if ever I returned home. I knew it would not be long before they started to call me the boy who lost. I failed a whole country, and I knew there was no recovering from that.

The next day, I decided never to swim again. I had discovered that swimming brought me nothing but pain and thus was no longer beneficial to me. I called my parents, who sounded very worried, and assured them that I was fine. They wanted me to speak to Coach Arnold, but I refused. I knew I could not stand to hear the voice of a man who taught me how to swim ever since I was a young boy. I tried my best not to break down over the phone as I told my parents I would not be coming back home. I didn't tell them where I planned on moving to, but I promised to give them my new cell number once I got to my destination. My mother did not make a fuss when I told them this, and I was glad they finally understood me.

CHAPTER THIRTY-FOUR

I settled down in a tranquil town in Italy where I was certain no one would remember me. My first night in Italy was terrible as I tried to kill myself again but stopped midway when I remembered how devastated my mother would be if I did. I cried myself to sleep for two straight nights before turning to alcohol. Alcohol became my new best friend and I turned to it every minute I felt sad. It was my coping mechanism that still allowed me the luxury of having some happy moments. I soon noticed that whenever I was not drinking the memories of my past would come to haunt me.

I was tempted to start dealing drugs but stopped when I thought of my parents, who assumed I was living the life of a king in Italy. I lived through late 20s and early 30s like this and even got arrested a couple of times. I could not keep a job because I was always drinking. I became a very crazy clubber and never slept at night; thus, I spent most of my nights at clubs dancing my sorrows away. Things spiraled out of control when I saw two of my friends from high school on the television. They were both successful and already had kids. It made me reflect on my life and wonder if I really could do better with my life.

Things did not change for me until the year I decided to go back home. My father and mother had both fallen ill at the same time. I felt it was a ruse to get me to return home until a nurse called me from a very famous private hospital and informed me that my parents had been admitted there. I flew down the moment I heard this news and did not for once stop to think of the fact that I was returning to a place I promised myself never to return to again. When I got to the hospital, I was told my parents had cancer. It was the strangest thing ever, and I laughed a lot because it had felt like an expensive prank to me. I wondered how cancer could attack two family members at once and believed it was not fair. My parents were very lovely people, and I knew neither of them deserved cancer. I was so scared for them that I first went to rehab to get better so I could take care of them. I am still always grateful that I was able to take care of them. I helped manage the bakery and my father's gadget store. I was also able to expand and build more stores across the United States. My parents were so pleased and proud of me that they died smiling. My father was the first person to die before my mother followed shortly after. They could not do without each other, and I loved that about them. I was happy that they had finally gotten the chance to see Star, who had left so early.

The next couple of months had me going back to therapy, and I was made to open up about every single thing I was feeling and had felt. I was made to understand that I never really healed and that was why I kept blaming myself for the deaths of Star and Cindy. It took many daily reaffirmations for me to finally believe that I was not the cause of their death. I stopped beating myself up daily, and I discovered that I started to sleep better. I also tried to get in touch with most of my friends from high school, and they were all happy to hear from me. I had expected awkward silence and blame when I called them, but instead, I received a warm reception with promises of them coming back to visit. This, however, never happened, but still, we all kept in touch. It felt wonderful to keep my old friends and make new ones again. I was also able to deal with the death of my parents better than I did with that of my sister and girlfriend. It was not like I finally accepted the phenomenon of death; I feel the fact was that I was able to accept their deaths, which made the blow a bit softer for me. I had worked towards making their last few months on Earth a memorable one, and I knew they died happy because I had fulfilled all their wishes. I still lost more people after my parents, but I was able to continue living despite this. I decided not to marry but instead focused all my attention on my businesses. I became the godfather of some of my friend's children and even contemplated the idea of adoption but never got around to it.

EPILOGUE

My old bones shook as I tried to walk towards the pool. Every step of mine seemed calculated as I stared at the swimming pool. I felt like a long-lost lover who finally found her love again. I had been able to overcome my fear of swimming. It had been years since I last swam, and as I looked at the water, I wondered if it missed me as much as I missed it. I smiled and dived into the pool.

Water became a love, a love that I could never live without.